I0622972

AMERICA

THE EAGLE HAS FALLEN

GORDON BALLANTYNE

SEVERED PRESS
HOBART TASMANIA

AMERICA: THE EAGLE HAS FALLEN

Copyright © 2019 Gordon Ballantyne

WWW.SEVEREDPRESS.COM

All rights reserved. No part of this book may be reproduced or transmitted in any form or by any electronic or mechanical means, including photocopying, recording or by any information and retrieval system, without the written permission of the publisher and author, except where permitted by law. This novel is a work of fiction. Names, characters, places and incidents are the product of the author's imagination, or are used fictitiously. Any resemblance to actual events, locales or persons, living or dead, is purely coincidental.

ISBN: 978-1-925840-67-4

All rights reserved.

CHAPTER 1

Just another typical day in the Robertson household. The sun is up early in Western Washington and James Robertson arises to start another work day as a homebuilder in Gig Harbor. He is a tall, distinguished looking, well-built forty-five-year-old starting to show his age. Streaks of silver are starting to invade his red tinted goatee and gravity is slowly reducing a muscled chest while simultaneously expanding his mid-section; "from a six pack to a pony keg;" he thinks quietly to himself. His full head of hair is fortunately blond so the occasional grey hair is not overly noticeable. His steely blue eyes examine himself in the mirror after his hot shower and determine that the two days of beard growth can go another day without attention. It is the same routine every day, a visit to the bathroom for the three "S's", a visit to the kitchen to load up on coffee, a visit to the job site in his pick-up truck to check on progress and an afternoon of annoying paperwork. Home by 6PM for dinner, a short playtime with his four-year-old daughter and a few stories to read at bedtime.

Nothing much changes in "The Harbor," the streets are mostly barren at 6 AM with the exception of the fleets of Econoline work trucks making their daily pilgrimage to worksites emblazoned with their representative companies. The bucolic town does not start seeing much activity until 9 AM when the Starbucks drive-through backs up around the block with high-end SUV's driven by ponytailed moms in yoga pants after the morning school drop off choreography at the various children's academies that dot the landscape around the Harbor.

Gig Harbor is an old, sleepy Croatian fishing village just west of the City of Tacoma across the Tacoma Narrows waterway in Washington State. It is accessible by two bridges built side by side to handle the flow, one old; rebuilt after its predecessor "Galloping Gurdy" plunged into the gorge during a severe windstorm and a new one built to meet the demands of the growing rural areas of the Peninsula. Gig Harbor's primary industry was always commercial fishing and the harbor is still riddled with old purse seiners that used to trek to Alaska for fishing season until the government stepped in to "regulate" the industry, making small family run fishing boats akin to the buggy whip industry. The waterfront promenade is littered with old dilapidated boat sheds and net sheds, there are still commercial fishing boats that operate out of Gig Harbor but the fleet is dwindling as government quotas, licensing requirements and safety regulations are rising faster than the will of the aging local fisherman to keep up or care. There was a time when every young local Gig Harbor teenager spent many a summer season "on the boats" to learn the trade and toughen them up for the realities of life; now helicopter parents would not dream of sending their precious children to sea. The boats are not equipped with wi-fi, cell service or medical personnel to squelch a sniffle. Everyone does not get a trophy on a fishing boat. Gig Harbor is on the Olympic Peninsula right at its fulcrum point, it boasts miles of coastline and hundreds of waterfront homes. The population of Gig Harbor is aging as evidenced by the fleet of Cadillac land yachts, driven by the blue hair crowd, that make the pilgrimage to the post office every day to check for their snail mail, talk to Trudy and Monica, the postal workers about their current medical maladies and speak to each other about local events and how the harbor has changed while waiting for their personal commune with Trudy and Monica. This is all done at top volume due to hearing loss; a rock concert has a similar decibel level. 10 AM is when the post office opens and every sane person under the age of 60 does not go anywhere near downtown at this hour. The entire Gig Harbor police department is scrambled to provide traffic control for the post office at 10 AM to stop the situation from deteriorating into a Cadillac bumper car carnival.

It is summer time and the air is rank with a smoky haze. Four huge wildfires are running rampant in northern British Columbia and to the east in the Cascade Mountains. The air quality, checked with alacrity every morning by my wife is permanently stuck on red. Our healthy four-year-old daughter spends most of the night coughing with her small respiratory system stung by the acrid smoke. We have air conditioning in our rural home but it is mentally and physically exhausting to keep a four-year-old only child occupied all day in a house. Our house is 4,000 square feet and every room seems like a playroom with trinkets, toys and "kid stuff" strewn everywhere. Grandparents seem to take great delight in purchasing the latest toys for their little "Toots;" I have learned to wear slippers full time in the house as there is nothing quite as painful than stepping on a plastic Lego with bare feet. We have ten acres for the little one to roam with her two furry friends; Caymus, a Rhodesian Ridgeback and Hunter, a French Bulldog. A Rhodesian Ridgeback is a large dog, red wheaten in color with a distinctive ridge of hair on their spine that grows against the grain of the rest of their coat so it looks like their hackles are permanently up. It is rumored that Rhodesians were originally used as big game lion hunters in Africa; ours, however, must be from a different genetic line since he enthusiastically chases our local bunny population until the rabbit drops a few turds and the dog stops to sample the apparently scrumptious emissions. A French Bulldog is a different sort of genetic hodgepodge and serves little purpose but to sit on laps and wheeze like a 70-year-old after aqua jazzersize at the local YMCA.

We have experienced a dry spell in "the land of perpetual rain" this summer with over 60 days of hot temperature in a row. This followed the worst wet winter and spring that had previously ever been recorded. It seems like the new normal for weather events starts with "the worst ...or... ever recorded," they say an iceberg the size of Delaware just broke off the Larson Ice Shelf and is floating around the Arctic. The talking heads, ie. Presidents and former Vice Presidents can't seem to agree whether Global Warming is a hoax generated by China or the end of the world as we know it.

"It's going to be a hot one" I think to myself as I back out of the garage and remember to load up some lawn sprinklers and hoses from the overwhelmed shelves of construction supplies I have in the garage. It is a constant struggle to try and keep the lawns green at our model home in a small subdivision we are building close to downtown Gig Harbor. It is a small family enterprise, I build the houses and my wife, a real estate agent, sells them. We have carved out a living within our community while large national, publically traded, housing giants carve the rest of the city into cookie cutter tracts of housing. Fortunately, in the "Harbor," you are either from here or "not"; my wife is a third generation harborite with Croatian roots so she is always welcome anywhere as the locals are all within three degrees of separation from the rest. Harbor people have a particular carriage and stroll that makes them instantly recognizable and a scowl that can spot an outsider instantaneously. The distrust from the government fishing debacle and any "outsiders" still permeate the citizenry. They would rather buy local than become some lot number and have their money sent to Texas in purchasing a new home.

I pull into the job site and review the previous day's progress while setting up for the current day's activities on the schedule. It is not overly demanding since I have been doing it all my life and all of my subcontractors have worked with me for years. I see that there is a truss boom truck arriving later in the morning so I make sure the area is clear and settle into my first cup of coffee for the day, waiting for the small flock of contractor vans to arrive and their inevitable barrage of questions, issues to be solved and work to be reviewed. I know it is going to be a good morning when I recognize all the vans and people exiting them since they are my usual crews and know the established program and protocols so reeducation is not going to be on my morning menu.

The truss truck arrives a little early but we are ready for it. Trusses are the large pre-made roof rafters that are boomed up onto the house structure so they can be assembled into a roof. They are assembled like a jigsaw puzzle. The boom truck sets up its large outriggers and the operator chains up the first large bundle to be lifted into the air. The crane surges under the load and the trusses begin to arc into the air. The large package of trusses is poised over the roof and slowly begins its descent and…STOPS!

I quickly hop out of my truck and all I hear is silence. No trucks, drills, saws, nail guns or motors running. The sounds of progress on any construction site. I am staring up at the suspended trusses in the sky and all I see is an azure glow in the sky that reminds me of the Northern Lights. All of the workers come out of the houses they are working on and start checking electrical connections and breakers, trying to figure out why their tools have stopped working. Nothing…Lights are out everywhere and even stranger still, all the cars and trucks out on the busy road by my project's entrance have gone still and silent. I grab my cellphone to call my wife and am greeted with a blank screen. Thinking I have let the battery die I plug it into my truck's charger and…nothing. I try to start my truck and…nothing. Wow, absolutely nothing works. I stand next to my truck and slowly watch the trusses poised above my house frame start to slowly descend as the hydraulics that hold the boom elevated start to lose their built-up pressure. This is real. The only explanation I can come up with is Solar Flare like the Carrington or some form of EMP; a high altitude nuclear blast sending an influx of electrons to overpower the electrical grid and fry all types of electronic devices. Almost everything today has a microprocessor chip installed in it or runs on electricity. If the grid was fried then we would be in deep trouble.

All the workers were coming to me asking what was up. As the developer and general contractor, I was the boss and all the workers were looking to me for guidance.

"What the hell?" asked a plumber named Randy. "It looks like your power is out and my darn work truck won't start."

"Well…" I replied, "It seems like everything electrical or electronic is out."

"What the hell are we supposed to do?" Many are now asking as they join the conversation.

"My advice for all of you is to gather all the food and water you have in your trucks and start making your way home," I answered the crowd. "There has been some kind of electrical event and while I hope it is some type of local power surge, I think this is more widespread. I have a case of water in the back of my truck and you are all welcome to some. Those of you with packs should load them up and I have some plastic garbage bags and duct tape for those of you who don't. I have a few wheelbarrows on site and a few wheeled carts that you can load up to make the journey easier."

"I live 100 miles from here," Randy the plumber complained. "How the hell am I supposed to get that far?"

"There is now a limited number of options for transportation," I replied. "Horsepower now only comes from horses. There might be some older vehicles without electronics in them still running but the bridges will be blocked with stalled cars so that leaves horses. The other most efficient mode of transportation currently available will be bicycles. I will not condone theft so that leaves you with bartering or trading things of value for what you need. The most valuable items in the coming months will be bullets, beans and band-aids. Fortunately, all of you working here have marketable trade skills and the ability to work hard so if you are smart then you will survive what is coming. I will give you some pointers from some things I have read about situations like this…

"Step 1. Secure a water source. Water is life that covers everything from drinking it to watering crops and livestock. Almost all water is pumped either out of wells to municipal systems or out of wells directly into houses. The large water towers that you see in small cities will go dry or not have enough water in them to provide pressure to the system within days without the pumps working to fill them. Homes that are on wells need power to pump water into houses. That leaves solar power or wind power to pump water out of the earth. You can find emergency supplies in your hot water tanks but I recommend filling every available container, including bathtubs, as soon as possible to retain this valuable resource. Water taken from lakes and streams will need to be filtered, boiled or treated before drinking as there will be no medicine available in the coming months. Water can be harvested from flowing water like streams or springs via a hydraulic ram pump or Archimedes screw to lift the water, those items can be assembled using specialty plumbing parts and fittings.

"Step 2. Secure a food source. The average house has three days of food on hand and the average grocery store has the same. In three days, people will be hungry, in six they will be starving. You can go up to three weeks without food before dying and three days without water before doing the same. You therefore have six days to get out of any population source larger than ten thousand people and move closer to a source of food and water. City folk have no clue how to grow, hunt or forage for food, they all think it just comes from the grocery store. After three days the strong will start to take from the weak via force.

"Step 4. Medicine. They are no longer making it. Antibiotics, antipsychotics, insulin, and pain medicine just became life and death commodities. They will literally be worth their weight in gold. People usually have a few left-over antibiotics in their medicine cabinets because they did not take the full course proscribed usually putting themselves at greater risk from the original infection. Over the counter fish antibiotics are made of the same active ingredient so they will work in a pinch. Antibiotic or antibacterial topical creams are also of value since a large cut just became a potential life threatening situation. The hospitals and doctors you rely on just became very hard to find and utilize.

"Step 5. Defense. Whatever supplies you and your loved ones manage to procure just became commodities and either the desperate or despotic will try and take them from you. Do not trust anyone."

All I could think about was my wife and little "toots." I had to get home. My wife is not a wilting daisy but she is definitely "fancy" and enjoys the finer things in life. I have grudgingly become a "prepper" over the last few years based on my belief that the government has become more and more in control of people's lives while people have become more dependent on the government in living their lives. The delicate balance of power has swung from independence to dependence. I subscribed to the more Reganesque stance of, "Government is not the solution to the problem, government is the problem." Whether it be global warming, nuclear bad actors, EMP, pandemic or government debt; the government would be so overwhelmed by the needs of the people in a disaster situation that it could not respond to a mere sliver of disaster. The government response to Hurricane Katrina in New Orleans was a wake-up call for me as I sat watching the anarchy and misery in the "Big Easy" while the government tried ineptly to respond. New Orleans looked like a third world country. Many people or "sheeple," as they were referred to, died waiting for the government to save them rather than focusing on saving themselves and their loved ones. It made me angry but it was also a personal call to action. I was woefully unprepared to survive a disaster: I only had the standard three days of food in our pantry, my individual house well was grid powered and I did not own a gun or know how to safely operate one. I was basically subordinating my responsibility to myself and my family to the government.

Some workers at the job site followed my recommendations and began the long trek home. Others elected to stay at the job site and wait for either the power to be restored or someone to come help them. I walked over to my truck and pulled out my "three-day pack" and began getting dressed in my "long walk" gear. I have packed and repacked this VVV emergency three-day bug out bag so many times over the years that I know every piece of equipment in it, how to use it and when to use it in different situations. The job site is fortunately only ten miles from my home so the journey would not be onerous and hopefully not be dangerous either. I have planned for a situation like this but the reality may be different than I envisioned. Randy the plumber looked over at me and came walking over.

"Heading home?" he asked somewhat sheepishly.

"Yes but I'll take a longer route around to stop at a few stores that probably have some supplies I will need," I replied evasively.

"Want company?" he asked with determination.

"Don't you need to get home to your family?"

"I don't have a family, my wife left me a few years ago and we did not have any kids, so I don't have much to get back to," Randy said frankly.

I looked at Randy closely. He was mid 40ish like myself, a little on the short side and balding on top. He was pretty trim due to the hard work and was always easy to get along with at the job site. I knew I could not survive alone at my homestead but I also knew that additional mouths to feed in the coming months would need to be balanced by the work and defense output of anyone added to my household.

"I tell you what, let's get packed up, head over to my place and see how we do," I said, passing judgement in my mind that Randy's skills as a plumber would be useful in the future and his positive mental attitude would be a benefit.

"Do you need anything from the plumbing truck?" asked Randy hopefully.

I went over to the fully stocked plumbing truck and made Randy a quick diagram of a hydraulic ram pump. He had all the necessary one-way valve parts and fittings to assemble one. He pulled all the pieces together to build a ram pump on the truck's workbench. "How does it work and how many do you want?" he asked helpfully.

"As many as you can carry of the critical one-way check valves," I responded. "Those parts will be invaluable over time since they represent the only way to lift water. I have a spring fed creek on my property and we might need the added water volume for irrigation. The pump works by sending water down a drive pipe where its force and pressure will close a one-way valve creating a hammer effect. The hammer effect creates energy which backflows into the large PVC chamber, building pressure. The second one-way valve stops the water flow into the water line until there is enough pressure in the PVC chamber to open the valve. The elevation drop, length and size of the drive pipe determines how high and far you can move the water depending on the size of the pump."

Randy fashioned a backpack out of a few burlap sacks that plumbing fittings come in. "Tools?" he asked.

"I have a full set at the house," I replied thoughtfully. "Our priority is water fittings and any special tools needed to join them that do not involve electricity. I have a bunch of PEX water pipes at my house but haven't been able to use it since I don't have the magic special tool to join the pipes."

Randy took a short time in filling his sack and locking up his truck. He grabbed some paint supplies that the painter had left next to his truck and began eliminating all his company logos identifying his truck as a plumbing vehicle. "We might need something left here in the future so there is no sense in advertising our stash."

"Smart," I replied. "I guess we had better get going. Hey wait, do you have any silver brazing rods?"

"Yes I do, those things are expensive. Do we need to braze joints instead of using solder?" Randy asked. Brazing is a way to join pipes end to end versus soldering which involves one pipe fitting over another, using flux to draw solder into the joint after heating it.

"No but the rods are almost pure silver and silver and gold may become the only currency available for trade other than bullets," I replied, thinking years into the future if money ever had value again.

Randy grabbed two full bundles of silver brazing rods and added them to his sack. "Where to?" he asked with a jump in his step.

"We are going to the feed store," I replied. "They will have everything we need for the future. Most people will be heading to the food stores or pharmacies to stock up on emergency supplies. It will probably be a disaster area by tomorrow as the reality of the situation sets in. We will be looking to the future since the only source of food will be what you can produce. The side trip will add another ten miles to our journey but it will be well worth it in the long run and enhance our ability to survive."

We set off to the feed store with the afternoon sun starting to heat up. Multiple people on the roadways were still walking around their vehicles with the hoods up staring at their engines as if willing them to start. "Try it again," was the most common phrase we heard from husbands buried under the hoods of their cars asking their wives or children to give the starter one more try. Small groups of people were gathered at the ends of driveways asking each other what was happening. Randy and I just kept walking along, minding our own business. My comfortable "walking clothes" were comprised of 511 khaki pants, hiking shoes and a neutral colored long sleeve shirt untucked to cover up my Glock 19 MOS 9MM pistol tucked into the waistband of my pants in a conceal carry holster. I had applied for and received my conceal carry permit years prior by submitting myself to the required government background check. It was a small price to pay in my personal time to get fingerprinted and have a background check performed in exchange for the security of being armed and able to defend myself and my family.

"Seems everyone is just standing around waiting to be told what to do," was Randy's observation as we passed multiple groups. Randy was staying astride of me looking slightly comical with his burlap sack backpack and plumbing "outfit" of blue coveralls and work boots.

"There will only be predators and prey in the future," I replied wistfully. "People will either figure out how to survive or they will perish. The estimates that I have read suggest that in an event that I think we are experiencing, will result in the death of over 75% of the population in the next six months."

"You have to be kidding me," Randy replied aghast. "We live in the most advanced society in the history of the world. It is not possible."

"Well…" I replied. "Without access to pharmaceutical drugs like insulin, heart medications and antibiotics, over 10% of the population won't last a month. Without access to health care we will lose another 10%. The population centers will start to die off after three weeks since all the food for these areas is trucked in and there is not enough food to go around. Violence will claim another 30-50% as the strong start to prey on the weak. Existing food and water resources are finite and there is not enough to go around. If you do not have the ability to produce food and water and have the ability to defend what you produce then you will perish, plain and simple. It is now an ugly world out there and I hope humanity and good will prevail. I will hope for the best but plan for the worst."

I have constantly been looking at my gold watch which had belonged to my grandfather. He had purchased it when he retired as a millwright in a lumber mill. The Wittnauer was a wind-up watch that everyone constantly jives me about due to its antiquity and the requirement to wind it up. I guess the last laugh was on them since I know what time it is and they don't. I have been methodically counting our paces and adjusting a set of beads attached to a paracord in my hand.

"What the hell are you doing?" asked Randy.

"I am seeing how fast we are going and how far we have travelled using my ranger walking beads." I showed Randy my set of ten beads and five beads threaded through a paracord. "Every thirty paces equals one hundred feet and every time we complete the one hundred paces then I move one of the set of ten beads to the other end of the line. Once all ten are used then I move one of the five beads at the top and reset the ten beads at the bottom. When all five top beads are moved over then I know we have walked a mile. My watch tells me how long it took to walk the mile so I know how fast we are going."

"OK Mr. Fitbit for Noah," replied Randy with a grin. "How fast are we going? Or do you need to pull out your abacus to tell us?"

I laughed. "It is just a habit when hiking. We are moving at approximately 5 miles per hour and will get to the feed store by lunchtime. We can stop for lunch at the feed store since it looks like you have not skipped any meals recently based on your plumber's butt and waistline."

"Do you have any food at your place?" asked Randy.

"Shhh!" I replied forcefully, turning to him while bringing my index finger up to my lips. "The one thing you never want to talk about in any survival situation, where anyone can hear you, is about food. It will only make you a target. Don't worry Randy, I have you covered. You may lose your plumber's butt in the coming months but I can keep you fed."

We continued our trek, passing the jigsaw puzzle of cars in the road, both abandoned ones and others with people still inside waiting out the storm. Fortunately we only saw a few car and truck accidents since the tortoise paced twenty-five mile per hour speed limit in Gig Harbor was strictly enforced by the tacticool police force after their morning post office shift. I never quite understood why the Gig Harbor Police Force needed to be all geared up for World War III in their full battle dress every day since the biggest crime of the century in Gig Harbor was the mauling of the Mayor's PeekaPoo designer dog by an off-leash pit bull rescue who had escaped his yard. Sure enough we arrived at the feed store around noon. The parking lot was pretty empty and there were not too many customers in the store or lot. I went to the front doors and was pleasantly surprised to see the doors were still open. The inside of the store was completely dark but with the sunshine streaming through the front windows and the glow of the emergency exit battery backup lights, we could still see. We were greeted by a cashier as we entered.

"Hi!" said the attractive red headed clerk with a large name tag that read "Cindy" emblazoned on her ample chest. "We are only accepting cash or taking credit only if you already have a store account with us since all the tills are down. We are trying to get the forklifts operating but have been unsuccessful so we can't sell bulk feed at this time."

"No problem Cindy," I replied with a wave, recognizing her as one of the usual employees working the tills. "I have an in-store account. How late are you guys staying open?"

"We will probably be here until closing as usual," was Cindy's reply.

"Thanks," I said.

I turned to Randy, speaking to him quietly. "OK, here is the plan, you head to the clothing department and get yourself some comfortable clothes, a pack and walking boots. Then I want you to head to the seed department, buy as many vegetable and grain seeds you can find that say heirloom seeds on the packages. I also want you to pick up as many canning lids as they have, especially any reusable lids."

"OK," was his perplexed reply as he set off to the clothing section of the store That's what I always liked about Randy over the years. Some construction workers like to debate, moan or give excuses once clear directions have been given. You sometimes feel like a glorified babysitter on a construction site cajoling wayward children to complete their assigned work. Randy always figured out how to get your request done regardless of extra time or effort on his part without the usual bellyaching that comes with certain requests usually involving cleaning up after yourself. I went over to the marine department and started loading up on fish antibiotics in as many different types available using the flashlight from my pack to read the fine print. I then pushed my cart over to the "chicken" bins. These are the galvanized tubs in any feed store where the live hatchlings are located and my daughter's favorite stopping point in the store. I look at the different placards in front of the tubs and identify the two pens that have the heartiest outdoor breeds for our local climate and start filling up the cardboard containers provided by the store with the little chirping yellow puffballs; all tolled I get forty chicks and three large bags of feed. I also notice one bin off to the side and look in to see a rooster and a full grown chicken with "Free to a good home" tag on the bin. Most people with coops restock their chicks every few years and bring the leftover ones to the feed store since some breeds of chickens will kill hatchlings in the coop. I box up the two full grown ones as well. The trouble with chicks is most of them are guaranteed to be female and without a rooster we will not be able to expand our coop in the future. I meet up with Randy and take our hauls to Cindy's cashier stand.

"Wow!" she says surveying our carts. "You guys are going crazy this year with the chickens and garden."

"Well..." I replied evasively. "The store bought eggs you buy these days are starting to give me stomach troubles and the poultry produce just isn't that fresh anymore. The price is also through the roof since my wife insists on all the new aged organic stuff, they don't call it Whole paycheck Foods for nothing."

"Your total is $498 Mr. Robertson." said Cindy. "Management has allowed $750 for credit account holders and while I am sympathetic to your stomach issues, I would suggest you purchase some more feed for your chickens since those three bags will only last you around six months with forty little mouths to feed, even if you free range them. We are in a potential disaster scenario here and your stomach and wallet notwithstanding, I would suggest you take full advantage of management's generous credit terms for its long-term clients. Management feels that its inventory should go to people who can make good use of the store resources rather than people like say...the government."

"I'll take as many chicken feed bags as possible Cindy please," I replied, turning red with embarrassment.

"You have around ten acres out around Artondale don't you Mr. Robertson?" Cindy asked shyly.

"Um yes," I replied. I was now on high alert knowing that anonymity was paramount to safety.

"If hypothetically my husband, myself and two kids came to your house in my old 1979 pickup outside loaded up with chicken feed, some fencing and some more chickens, would you let us in?" Cindy asked hopefully. "We live over in a new housing community by Costco in Gig Harbor North and I don't think that's going to be a very good spot to ride out this storm."

"Tell me Cindy, are you a city girl or a country girl?" I asked, looking her directly in the eye.

"Pure country," Cindy laughed. "My husband is in the service and we have not been in contact but I know he will make it home. He is stationed at joint base Lewis McCord over by Tacoma and I know he will find me. I plan on leaving him a coded note at our small house with a meeting place."

"Does your pickup have a gun rack?" I asked, fishing a little deeper.

"Mr. Robertson, I can shoot out a squirrel's eye at 200 yards and my husband is an army ranger, good enough?" she said frankly.

"You pass." I laughed. An army ranger would be a huge asset to my homestead especially if his family was also steeped in the culture.

Just then I heard a commotion in the feed store parking lot. A large one ton dually 1978 ford pickup came rolling into the lot towing a large flatbed trailer. The bed of the pickup and trailer was bristling with armed men. I ducked behind the counter out of sight and pulled my 9mm handgun from its concealed holster.

"Cindy! Is there a back way out of the store?" I asked quickly trying to figure out an avenue of escape.

"Don't worry Mr. Robertson, that is Mr. Stutz, the owner of the store." Cindy laughed looking down at me behind the counter. "His bark is worse than his bite but we are not in any danger except from the occasional F-Bomb."

Mr. Stutz came walking into the store with three of his men, giving Cindy and me a look. "Any problems Cindy?" he asked while looking at my drawn handgun that was thankfully pointed at the floor.

"No problem at all Mr. Stutz," replied Cindy with a smile. "Mr. Robertson and I were just working out an arrangement."

"Good!" said Mr. Stutz. He came over and shook my hand. Mr. Stutz was a no-nonsense rancher with the bowlegged stance of a horseman. He looked to be in excellent shape and had that timeless appearance where you would not be surprised to find out if he was fifty or seventy years of age. His hands were like rough sandpaper and were no strangers to hard work. "Thank you for taking care of Cindy. The store might get a little hot in the near future and no place for a woman. I am loading up all my feed and seed and taking it to my farm. Thank goodness I kept the old Ford or I would have been stuck here. I have a few hundred acres out in Arletta and between the farm hands and security people I just don't have enough room to properly accommodate Cindy and her family. I was hoping Cindy would find a great home better suited to her two little 'uns. She is a hard worker and will be as much as an asset to you as she has been to me over the years. Cindy, I will cover the store, let's get you loaded up so you can go get your beautiful children to safety."

I knew Mr. Stutz had a large acre farm about 20 miles from my homestead so I quickly jotted down a note and handed it to him.

"What's this?" he asked, looking at the piece of paper proffered.

"It is my shortwave handle," I replied. "If you get your hands on a working radio you will be able to get ahold of me in the future."

"Thanks," he replied. "You seem to have all your shit in one bag and be quite a few steps ahead of the game. Let's hope this is all for drill but I think we both know it isn't. Please take good care of Cindy and I hope to be in touch with you once things settle down a bit." With that Mr. Stutz turned and started giving his hands orders to get organized and start loading up. I turned to Randy and Cindy suggesting we had best get moving since we were burning daylight and had a lot of things to do and not a lot of time to get it done. Randy and I started wheeling our carts down the street to begin our ten-mile journey home in the midday heat. Fortunately, most of the walk would be downhill and we should be home well before darkness hit.

Randy was pushing his cart next to mine. "Why heirloom seeds?" he asked pensively.

"Heirloom seeds grow true to form and most importantly, the seeds harvested from the fruits, grains and vegetables also grow true. Hybrid and genetically modified seeds were created to avoid common pests and resistance to certain blights but the seeds harvested from the hybrid plants typically do not propagate or grow as plentiful as the original seeds. Your yield can decrease over multiple generations of growing. Hybrid seeds were an avenue for seed manufacturers to keep farmers under their thumbs requiring them to keep purchasing seed annually rather than using part of their crop for future seeds. Many manufacturers did not even allow farmers to even try and reuse seeds from their crops and sued them for patent infringement if they did."

We continued walking and I pulled out a few granola energy bars from my pack and handed some to Randy. We also made sure to keep hydrated as I kept filling Randy's water bottle from my platypus water container on my pack, using the fill tube. We were both sweating profusely from the exertion and I kept my bandana in my hand to mop up the dripping sweat. We were almost halfway home according to my estimation and stopped for a water break, to wring out my saturated sweat rag and to get out of the oppressive June sun. There were cars broken down everywhere stopped haphazardly in the street, many of them with open hoods. We were watching two young girls riding their bikes up the street in the distance when we saw two men jump out from behind a car and violently push the two girls to the ground forcing them from their mountain bikes. One of the men was wielding a large machete that he waved menacingly in the faces of the two young girls while yelling at them to move away from the bikes. The men picked up the bikes and started riding towards us. They both looked like hoodlums with multiple visible tattoos and piercings. One of them looked like their face had fallen into my fishing tackle box as there were so many bits of metal sticking prominently out of his head. They spied us on the sidewalk and braked hard in front of us, blocking our path.

"What do you guys have in the carts and packs?" demanded the machete wielding jagwhistle with the pincushion face. He looked like a Goth Royal Dragoon on his trusty mountain bike steed waving his saber above his head.

"A fishing pole to go with the hooks in your face," I replied menacingly.

He looked at me wild-eyed and dismounted his recently purloined transportation device. "You're going to pay for that!"

as he started towards me on the sidewalk with his machete raised in the air.

He was coming directly from our front so I shoved the heavily laden cart towards him, catching him in the midsection before he could swing the machete. He was doubled over in front of my battering ram cart so I calmly pulled my Glock pistol from its holster and shot him in the head. A red mist erupted from the back of his head and he fell to the sidewalk like a poleaxed cow. His baldheaded partner dropped his bike and was scrambling on all fours, crab walking away from me, looking at my gun with wide eyes. I slowly walked up to him as he was crawling away from me and told him to freeze and not move a muscle, pointing my gun at his head.

"We were just trying to get home," he blubbered pitifully from the ground. "Honest Mister, please don't kill me. We didn't hurt anyone. Please sir, I have a family."

"Are you left or right handed?" I asked calmly while keeping my pistol aimed at his head.

"Right," the quivering thief replied.

I stepped up to the bike thief and brought the heel of my boot down hard on his left hand that was on the sidewalk. I heard multiple bones snap in his hand. The thief yowled in pain rolling onto his back while cradling his injured hand.

"You are now marked as a thief," I said menacingly. "I should shoot you where you stand but it is a waste of a bullet. If I ever see you again, I will shoot first and ask questions later. You can also haul your buddy into the woods over there." I walked over and put the machete in my cart and watched the bald-headed hoodlum struggle to pull his ex-friend off the sidewalk with his remaining good hand. The two girls who had been knocked off their bikes approached us cautiously after seeing the confrontation from afar. One of the teens was cradling her arm protectively to her chest.

"Thanks Mister," one of the teens said with tears streaming down her face in a gushing torrent. "They just came out of nowhere and pushed us off our bikes. We were so scared we did not know what to do."

"Let me see that arm," I said gently while taking off my pack and pulling out my first aid kit.

The injured girl gingerly offered her arm for inspection. It had an obvious fracture in her forearm ulna.

"How far are you guys from home?" I asked gently.

"We live about five miles that way," the uninjured girl answered, pointing in the direction Randy and I were going.

"Ok," I said, pulling out a triangle bandage and putting the injured girl's arms in a sling and gave her a couple of Ibuprofen tablets and a drink of water to wash them down. I directed the uninjured girl to walk the bikes while the injured girl walked beside her. "We are heading in that direction so why don't you girls walk on ahead of us, that way we can make sure you get home safe."

"Jesus!" Randy exclaimed with wide eyes. "What the hell just happened?"

I held up my finger for a second and took a few steps into the woods next to the sidewalk and promptly threw up the energy bar I had just eaten behind a tree. Fortunately the two girls did not see me but the bald-headed thief did and started pulling his comrade even faster away from me into the woods. I was pretty sure we would not be seeing him again. I took a long swig of water to clean out my mouth. "I saw him as a threat so I put him down. I figured he would quickly graduate from petty theft to murder pretty quickly once he figured out the police were not coming anymore. I did not want him anywhere near my neighborhood."

"Good call," said Randy nodding his head. "That was one hell of a shot, you hit him right between the eyes."

"It would have been a great shot if that was where I was aiming. Unfortunately I was aiming for his chest, aim small miss small is what I have always been taught." I laughed, trying to erase the memory of the hoodlum's head exploding like a ripe melon. "That was the first time I have ever shot at a person."

I have practiced shooting at stationary paper targets for years and I was amazed at the difference between that and a living breathing moving target. We continued down the street following the two girls in front of us after I was done rinsing out my mouth. After about four miles the girls stopped at a long driveway in the tree line abutting the main road about a half block from the turn to my house.

"Thank you again sir, this is Mary's house and I live just next door," the uninjured girl said, turning to us while still holding the two bikes. "We were so scared when those guys grabbed us. We thought they were going to kill us or do something worse. I am still shaking."

"What were you guys doing so far from home?" Randy asked.

"We were coming home from school," the injured girl replied. "When the lights all went out and the power went down our teachers kept us locked down in the school. We knew our parents would be home so they let us ride our bikes together like we always do. It is only a seven-mile ride so we thought it would be safer for us to just ride home than wait for our parents to have to walk and get us."

Just then a short fireplug of a lady with severe cropped hair came barreling down the driveway, yelling at Randy and me to get away from her daughter. We did look a little out of place, like a couple of urban hobos pushing our shopping carts down the road, stopping at her driveway to talk to the teenage girls.

"Mom...Wait!" said the injured girl.

"What happened to you?" cried the mom when she spotted the girl's arm in a sling, looking at Randy and me accusingly. "What did you do to her?" she screamed while staring daggers at me.

"Whoa! Slow your roll," I said, stepping back as the mama bear inserted herself in front of her wounded cub. "We were just trying to help."

"Well help yourself down the road," she said dismissively.

"Easy mom," the injured girl said. "A couple of really scary guys knocked us off our bikes while we were riding home. One of them had a machete! They threatened us and took off on our bikes. These two stopped them, took our bikes back and walked us home. These two men saved us."

"Oh," the lady said, deflating slightly from full blown bulldozer mode. "I guess I owe you two an apology. I was out of my mind with worry when the power went out and the car wouldn't start. My husband works in town and I didn't know what to do. Thank you so much for saving my daughter."

"No problem," I said. "Your daughter has a broken arm and the bones will need to be set. I don't know if there is a doctor nearby but the arm should be set sooner rather than later so it knits properly. The hospital is fifteen miles away and is probably overrun with problems right now and will not be a safe place, especially since they have lost power. Most have emergency backup generators but if those were fried too then it will be bedlam around there and not a safe place. I live just up the street and can set it in an emergency if needed."

"I do not know if there is a doctor in the neighborhood," she said pensively. "Please, come up to the house, I have been home all day and would like to thank you properly with a cup of coffee."

"Thank you for the offer Ma'am," I replied. "But we need to get home. I live about five blocks from here over that way and will be happy to check on your daughter tomorrow once you and your husband have had the chance to sit down and figure out what you want to do with your daughter's arm."

"Any idea what is going on out there? I am Miriam by the way."

"I don't know," I replied, shaking my head. "I think there has been an electrical event, either an EMP or Electro Magnetic Pulse or a CME, a Coronal Mass Ejection. It is the only reason I can think of why the grid is down and electronic devices are not working."

"When will they get the power back up and running?" Miriam asked.

"I don't honestly know," I replied. "But if the event was large enough to fry all electronics and depending on its location, the power might not be restored for years."

"Oh my!" Miriam gasped, putting her hands up to her mouth. "What are we going to do? My husband is a lawyer for the City of Gig Harbor."

"I would suggest sheltering in place depending on the resources you have at hand and working with your friends and neighbors on how to stay safe. The local government may have a disaster plan in place but either way your husband will probably be very busy in the next few days," I replied. "I may be overreacting but it is better to be safe than sorry in the coming days. Stay off those bikes and put them away where people can't see them. There are a lot of people stranded out there and a bicycle will be a very attractive target in the next few weeks."

"Thank you again for your help," Miriam said solemnly.

"No problem," I replied. "I will come check on you tomorrow."

Miriam watched us go as we started pushing our carts down the road. Randy and I continued down the road a few blocks until I saw that Miriam had turned back into her driveway.

"We need to turn back and go up that road we just passed," I told Randy.

"Why?" asked Randy.

"Because I did not want Miriam to see where we went," I replied. "I don't know her and the first rule of safety in these types of situations is not letting anyone know where you live. Security is paramount to staying safe and the safest place to be is where nobody knows you are there."

"How are we going to do that?" asked Randy.

"You'll see in about five minutes," I replied with a wink. "You do know what killed the cat don't you?"

Randy and I backtracked one street and began pushing our carts up the hill. Most of the houses off our street are on acre tracts like Miriam's. We turned into a cul-de-sac development with newer houses lining both sides of the street.

"Nice houses," observed Randy. "Which one is yours?"

"None of the above," I replied with a wink.

"We aren't going to turn around again are we?" Randy asked with a whine. "That was a steep hill we just came up."

"See that dirt road at the end of the cul-de-sac?" I asked. "We go down there."

We continued through the six house cul-de-sac to two mailboxes at the end of the road abutting a gravel driveway. I promptly stopped and removed both boxes and tossed them into the woods. We meandered down the gravel path for around two hundred feet until we came to a house nestled in the woods.

"Here?" asked Randy.

"Nope," I said with a smile. "Turn right onto the paved driveway past this house."

We turned and came to an aluminum electric gate with an adjoining wooden fence.

"This is us," I said. "My house is around the corner. That is my neighbor, Amy's house we just passed."

We continued up the drive until my house was visible. It is a four thousand square foot craftsman two story house sitting on five acres. I own another adjoining five acres that is all dense woods. Amy at the foot of the drive has an additional five acres next to me that is also wooded. Our two dogs Caymus and Hunter came running down the driveway barking at us until we approached. Caymus is a Rhodesian Ridgeback and looks fairly menacing as he comes running up to us, Hunter is simply wheezing, following behind trying to catch his breath. Upon identifying me they stopped and started wagging their tails, sniffing our carts and taking particular interest in Randy. We continued up the driveway and were greeted at the patio with my wife Belle carrying her twelve gauge shotgun.

"Hi Honey...I'm Home," I called out with a smile and a wave.

"Damn dogs gave me a heart attack." She laughed when she saw us. "I was pretty sure it was you but you never know."

The great thing about Rhodesian Ridgebacks is they are not yappers that bark at everything. They are fiercely protective of their family and home and only bark when the situation warrants it. You can tell by the tone of their bark if it represents "I'm unsure and checking it out" or "intruder alert." Having a big dog is often the best security system possible but being anonymous is even better. You can't steal what you can't find.

"Honey," I said to my beautiful wife of fifteen years. "This is Randy. He is a puppy that followed me home. Can I keep him?"

My wife laughed. She is a thin beautiful blonde with steely blue eyes. I married way out of my league but they say everyone needs a project and I thank my lucky stars every day that I am hers.

"Well, you'd better come in. More importantly, what did you bring me?" she asked, looking at our carts.

"Chicks!" I said cheerily.

"They had better not be blondes," she said.

"Nope," I replied. "They are more yellow colored. We also picked up a rooster just in case."

"Not another one!" she said with a smile. "It took me three months to finally convince the last one we had to leave, waking my ass up at the crack of dawn every morning. I think he ended up at the neighbors' place because I recognize his morning yowl and he is always a half hour ahead of all the other damn things in the area. Come on in Randy, we'll get the chicks in the secondary baby coop and you can come get cleaned up and have a meal."

"Thank you ma'am," replied Randy sheepishly. "I really appreciate you letting me stay with you and your family.

"Give it a few days then tell me how you feel," Belle said with a smile. "It's not all it's cracked up to be."

Off in the distance we heard a car approaching our neighborhood. Other than Mr. Stutz's truck we had not heard or seen a working vehicle all day.

"Quick!" I said hurriedly. "Honey, get the chicks inside and give Randy your shotty. Randy, come with me."

The two of us ran down the drive and up the gravel road to the cul-de-sac and were happy to see Cindy waving from the driver's window with two heads peeking over the dash. I ran up making a cutting motion across my throat. Cindy turned the engine off.

"Pop it in neutral," I said in a rush. "Randy, get behind with me and push."

"Why?" asked Cindy. "I can drive."

"Cindy, everyone in the entire community heard your truck. We need to be very quiet and make sure nobody knows where it went. No brakes Cindy. Randy and I will push really hard down the initial slope to the creek and hopefully have enough momentum to get it up the other side."

Randy and I ran around to the rear of the truck and started pushing. Fortunately the truck made it up the incline on the other side of the creek from the downhill momentum. We pushed the truck behind a stand of trees by our neighbor's. Cindy stepped out of the truck and her two kids slid out behind her.

"Hi!" she said cheerily. "I am so glad I made it. This is my son Jacob who is thirteen and my daughter Ellie who is five."

Her son Jacob walked straight up to me, looked me in the eye and put his hand out. "Hi, I'm Jacob."

I gladly shook his hand and introduced him to Randy whose hand he also shook. "Welcome Jacob," I said. "I'm glad you are here."

Cindy waved me over and said quietly while tucking a 9MM Sig Sauer into her pants; "I loaded up all the firearms, ammo and food I had at the house, grabbed the kids from school and headed over here as fast as I could. I had to drive on the sidewalks most of the way here due to all the cars in the way and fortunately the kids were in the playground and came running when they saw me pull up. I have never been waved down and yelled to so many times in my life. I felt like a stripper walking past a construction site. I barely stopped to get the kids and high tailed it out of there as fast as possible, not stopping for anything until I got here."

"Let me guess," Randy asked wistfully. "Get back on that darn shopping cart."

"Nah," I said dismissively. "Let's see if the tractor works."

"Won't the noise be a problem?" Randy asked.

"I like how you are thinking Randy but listen. Hear all the generators running? They will mask the noise of our tractor for a few weeks until everyone runs out of gas."

The five of us walked up the driveway and were met by my wife in the same position as before with her Glock 19 now at her side. "Let me guess…" she said with a smile.

"Can I keep them? I promise to take care of them." I laughed heartily. "This is Cindy, Jacob and Ellie. Cindy is from the feed store and brought us lots of presents for the homestead."

"Hello," said Cindy to my wife. "Thank you so much for allowing us to stay with you. I promise we will pull our weight, at least until my husband gets here."

"You are most welcome," my wife said to Cindy, giving her a hug. "Anyone who can put up with my husband's bad jokes and paranoia is always welcome, besides we need some more estrogen around here to keep these boys in line."

"Mommy!" I heard a little voice from the living room door. "Can I come out now?"

"Yes Avery," my wife said with exasperation. "What did we talk about playing hide and seek?"

"But you didn't come find me!" we heard as my four-year-old daughter came trotting onto the covered patio from the living room, dragging her stuffed dinosaur Hatter behind her. "Daddy!" she screamed running toward me.

I scooped her up in a big hug. "Avery, this is Randy and Cindy and Cindy's kids, Jacob and Ellie. Can you say hello."

Avery marched right up to Ellie and said, "Do you like Dinosaurs?"

Ellie's head bobbed up and down in the affirmative.

"Good, then let's go play!" Avery said, taking Ellie in tow into the house with the two dogs following. They know the most likely source of dropped food and a free meal.

"Come on in Cindy," my wife said to Cindy. "I'll get you settled while the bellhops go get your things. Chop, chop boys or no tip."

Randy, Jacob and I went around to the side of the house to the three car garage doors and I pushed the wireless keypad on the exterior of one and the automatic door opener started to whine.

"What the hell?" Randy exclaimed. "You have power?"

I pointed up at the solar panels on the roof. I sat on the medium sized lawnmower with an attached bucket and turned the key…Nothing. "Darn," I said dejectedly then looked down. The tractor was still in gear. I dropped it into neutral and hallelujah the tractor started right up. I pulled the tractor and tow cart out of the garage and said a small prayer thanking the lord for saving my back in the future and motioned for Randy and Jacob to hop on the cart. We travelled down the driveway toward the gate. I pulled out my keyring and unlocked the gate from the control box and swung the gate open. I pulled the tractor up to the truck and started unloading duffel bags onto the tractor's trailer. One of them was very heavy and I strained to lift it.

"What does she have in here?" I asked Jacob. "Rocks?"

"No sir," answered Jacob. "Those are my dad's firearms."

I unzipped the bag and had a look inside. Good lord. I thought I had some nice firearms but I am a Piker compared to Cindy and her husband. "I think I am going to like your dad," I said to Jacob.

We loaded up the tractor as full as we could. I told Randy to stay with the truck and I would unload at the other end and I sat Jacob in the driver's seat and gave him instructions on how to operate the tractor. Jacob told me that his grandparents had a farm in North Carolina and that he had already been taught. We managed to get all the materials unloaded from Cindy's truck and I relocked the gate. Randy and I walked back to the house after Jacob had parked the tractor and closed the garage doors.

"This place is pretty secluded," Randy said while looking around the property. "You can't see a single house or road from up here."

"Let's hope it stays undiscovered. We are going to have a lot of work to do in the coming days and months," I said, thinking of all the defense, food and resource management we would have to prepare for. "Let's get a shower and some dinner and figure out where to go from here."

We went up to the house and my wife and Cindy were already working on dinner, each with an ever present glass of wine in hand. I knew we had a well-stocked wine cellar of "Mommy juice."

"OK," my wife said taking charge. "I have put Cindy in Blair's room, we will put Randy in the downstairs playroom and the kids will sleep in the bonus room. We will keep the guest room empty for now until my Dad gets here. The ladies will shower in the morning, the kids in the afternoon and you boys get the evenings."

We all sat down to dinner and I said Grace. "Thank you Lord for getting us home safe, meeting new friends and the meal we are about to receive together. Please watch over our families who are not here with us now and we pray that they can find their way home to us. Please watch out for our community, our state and America as we persevere through these trying times. Amen."

After dinner we enjoyed sharing a bottle of wine, getting to know each other and bone tired, we all went to bed.

CHAPTER 2

The morning came quickly. Fortunately everyone, except my wife, were early risers. We started in on breakfast that Cindy prepared and coffee while my wife started her "getting up" process which involved breakfast in bed hand delivered by me. After breakfast and my wife's appearance I sat everyone down to go over our plan for the day and week.

"Ok everyone," I began. "Our first responsibility is safety and defense. Everyone except the kids, from this point forward, needs to be armed at all times. Cindy, I will leave the decision on Jacob to you."

Cindy laughed. "Jacob, what are the four rules of firearm safety?"

Jacob replied by rote. "Treat every gun as if it is loaded. Keep your finger off the trigger until ready to fire. Do not point your gun at anything you are not prepared to shoot or kill. Know what is between you and your target and beyond."

I laughed back. "OK then. Everyone, including young Mr. Earp here, needs to carry a handgun with them at all times and have a rifle or shotgun nearby. The purpose of your handgun is to be able to fight your way back to your rifle if needed. If anyone shouts out an alarm, Avery and Ellie are to run to the upstairs bathroom, shut the door and lie down in the tub. Jacob is to guard the top of the stairs and loft area covering the stairs and front door. The adults are to run to the rally point where Belle met us at the corner of the house. That area offers us cover from three sides and the ability to get to cover from the fourth vector of attack. We will have a six-hour watch rotation for the adults at night time. One adult will be on the roof by the chimney with a sniper rifle and my night vision monocular while the second will be on the patio area with the dogs. The dogs will alert everyone if danger is approaching and consider the dogs barking as an alarm. If I yell fallback then Jacob will grab Avery and Ellie and take them to our rally point in the woods and the adults will follow giving the kids time to get to the rally point. This is just a house and not worth our lives. Our second priority is food production. It is early June so we need to get our field prepped and planted so we can get the crop in before the late fall monsoons and the first winter frost. We have some winter wheat seeds so if we can get the seeds in the ground in the next few days we will be OK. Our vegetable garden you saw is planted but we will need to make it much bigger for our second vegetable harvest. Once the primary field and garden are planted, we will have to construct a greenhouse with some materials I have so we can grow year round. The chicken coop will need to be expanded after that for the 80 chickens we have. Eggs and poultry will be our primary barter supplies and hopefully we can get some pigs, cows and horses. The chicks won't mature and start laying eggs for another five to six months. The coop will be Avery and Ellie's primary responsibility in collecting eggs, cleaning the manure for the garden and feeding the chickens. Now to resources, we have enough food for everyone but it is a finite emergency supply. Our goal needs to be to produce more than we use, nothing gets thrown away. We have a stock of canned goods and anything extra we produce will be canned for winter months. Any food waste will be composted for the garden and paper goods will be burned. The hot water and cooking are currently supplied by our five hundred gallon buried propane tank. That supply is finite so we will install our wood burning stove with hot water coil. We will install it on the patio and hopefully Randy can come up with a plumbing solution for hot water. Our electrical system is solar that powers a battery bank and inverter. In the summer time the battery banks stay full but in the fall and winter there is not enough sunshine to keep the batteries topped up. So we need to conserve energy during those months and we also need to use light discipline in the evenings. No lights on after dark, period. During the winter we will have to use our generator during daylight hours to charge the batteries. We will have to come up with a sound and exhaust solution for the generator. I have around fifty gallons of gas on hand so we will have to either scrounge up more gas from abandoned cars or convert the generator to run on wood gas. Since all cooking and heating will be done with wood, we need to put up around ten cords of wood to see us through the winter. We will start in on the adjoining five acres and hopefully clear a path so our forty-two-foot fifth wheel can be repositioned in the woods as a fallback position. The great thing about trailers is that they are self-sufficient and the major systems run on 9volt DC as well as 110AC. We will set up a fallback position and reposition supplies to that area or can use the second camp to expand our homestead as needed. I need to go look at a girl down the street's broken arm this morning but first we are going to have a weapon check and target practice."

The dishes were cleared and the adults all went to get their firearm gear. I took Randy to my gun safe and outfitted him with a 9MM Glock and Uncle Mike's hip holster. I also set him up with a Colt M4 AR-15 with red dot sight. "Ever shot before?" I asked.

"Not much," he replied sheepishly.

I grabbed four targets and set them up at 35 and 100 yards in the field. I lined everyone up and instructed them to pull their handgun, fire three shots at the 35 yard target then run to the rifle stand and fire six shots at the 100 yard target. I demonstrated with my Glock and Daniel Defense AR-15 putting all my shots on paper. Next was my wife. She calmly shot her Glock, putting all her shots in the black and went to the rifle stand, picked up her semi-automatic 12 gauge and shot three loads of buckshot obliterating the target, she reloaded with three shells of deer slugs and shot the frame apart. I cleared the firing line shooting a dirty look at my wife and reset new targets for Cindy. Cindy was a crack shot putting all her sig shots in the money rings, ran over to the rifle line, took up her H&K MP4 and fired six single shots in the money rings as well. Next was Randy. He stood at the firing line and pulled his new Glock and took aim at the target. Before I could yell out, he fired and dropped his pistol, sticking his left thumb in his mouth. I went over to Randy and looked at his thumb. His hands were so calloused that the "Glock bite" only tore off one of his callouses at the webbing between his thumb and index finger.

"Revolver guy," I laughed. "Suck it up buttercup, you are lucky you didn't break your thumb. You have to put both thumbs forward on a semi-automatic pistol, gripping it like this." As I demonstrated. "Nice and easy on the trigger, not yanking but pulling. Line up the sites putting the ball in the bucket. You will feel the trigger break point but don't anticipate the bang. Only reset the trigger to the breakpoint for your second shot." Randy put two out of three on "Paper" and went to the rifle line. He got into a decent firing stance, pulled the trigger and nothing. "Safety Randy," I said. Randy found the safety and managed to only hit the target two out of six times.

"You know Randy," I said after he had safed his weapon. "Some guys are rifle guys and some guys are shotgun guys."

I handed him my wife's shotgun and lo and behold he had the eye. Some people like lining up front and rear sights and some people prefer using their eye as the rear sight like done with a shotgun. Jacob was next. He stepped up to the firing line drew his Sig 9mm, took a half step to the left and fired three shots directly into the bull's eye. He ran over to the rifle table, picked up his suppressed H&K and put two three shot automatic bursts into the bull's eye. I've tried some competition shooting and never seen anyone be able to do that off hand. Prone or benched maybe but this kid not only has a handgun quick draw technique but can shoot an automatic three shot burst bull's eye group.

"Have many trophies?" I asked with a laugh.

"A few," he said beaming with pride. "My dad is a Ranger marksman and the father-son Army tournaments are pretty competitive. We won the Army wide competition last year. Dad shot a possible perfect score but I missed two."

"Two shots out of fifty?" I asked incredulously.

"Five hundred," was the modest reply. "The wind was a little tricky on the third day for the six hundred yard shots."

I shook my head in awe. "Well Randy, I have an over-under bird gun shotty you can have. We need to get going on our mission of mercy down the street. Jacob, please strip, clean and reload the firearms. Then all the lawn areas and bank need to stripped of grass and underlying topsoil with the tractor and placed in the lower field so we can till it all in for planting. Leave the raised flower beds so we can use those to fill the greenhouse."

"Yes sir," was the immediate answer. "You know sir, we have a six round tactical semi-automatic shotgun for Mr. Randy; we also have a quick reload bandolier. We use them for three gun competitions but I'm sure Mr. Randy would rather have six shots instead of two before reloading. It looks like he might need a few extra tries at the target."

"Thank you Jacob...and Cindy," I replied. "I'm sure it will be put to good use. Perhaps you could help Mr. Randy with some shooting tips in the future since you seem to be the best gun slinger on the property. I also bet you know how to reload ammunition and since I have the equipment, I'm sure you can be our armorer on top of your tractor chores."

Randy and I grabbed our packs and headed toward the neighborhood. One of our cul-de-sac neighbors was at our small creek with a bucket.

"Hi Mr. Jones," I said to the fifty year old balding portly man stooped over the creek trying to scoop water with a Home Depot orange five gallon bucket.

"Hi there," he replied dejectedly. "Darn electricity is still out and the stupid water is not working. I tried calling the power company and the darn phone is out and there is no cell service. I had to walk home from the office yesterday when my car wouldn't start. When are they going to get this crap working again?"

"I don't know," I replied evasively. "This is my friend Randy and he'll be staying with us for a while."

"Hi there," said Mr. Jones while shaking Randy's hand. "You boys going to war?" he asked looking at our rifles with his nose turned up. "You can't just go walking around the neighborhood with guns on display."

"Well sir," I replied reasonably. "The Constitution and Washington State law says we can. We are just trying to be safe."

"Well, as the Homeowner's Association President, I will have to bring it up at the next board meeting," he said with authority. "We can't have people just walking around with brandished guns scaring people half to death."

"Sir, these guns are not only for our own personal safety but potentially yours as well. I'll overlook the fact that you are on my property and drawing water from my creek but please understand we are all in this boat together and only together will we get through it. Good day sir," I said dismissively while walking away, purposefully turning my back on him.

"Dumbass," said Randy when we were out of earshot. "Doesn't he know there is at least fifty and probably one hundred gallons of water in his hot water tanks?"

"Nope," I replied thoughtfully. "We will just keep our distance from Mr. Jones and his ilk. He doesn't have an inkling and there are three inklings in a clue. They will sit around on their asses and wait for somebody else to solve their problem for them and will unfortunately be in the third wave to die."

"Third wave?" Randy asked with raised bushy eyebrows.

"The first wave will be those in hospitals and on life saving medications, the second will be through violence as food and water is no longer available and the third will be during the winter when there is no food and the strong will start preying on the weak."

"Is there a fourth?" asked Randy in anticipation.

"Unfortunately, yes," I replied ruefully. "That will be when the strong groups of takers band together to form large gangs that will eliminate any communities that are not sufficiently strong enough to repel and defeat them."

"What are we going to do?" Randy asked in distress.

"We are going to survive," was my reply.

We walked down to Miriam's house and stopped mid driveway as I hailed "Hello the house." Miriam peeked out the front window and saw it was us.

"Thank goodness you are here, please come in," she said with worried eyes. "My husband is still not home and there have been a lot of strangers coming up to our house asking if we had any food or water. Some of the men saw my daughter and were giving her the eye. I told them that my husband was behind me with a shotgun and they need to get off my property. I don't know what to do."

"Don't worry Miriam, you did the right thing," I said. "Did you find a doctor for your daughter's arm?"

"No," she replied in anguish. "I gave her a couple of Percocets for the pain and she is pretty out of it. Can you please help her?"

"Of course. I am not a doctor but have some medical training and know what we need to do," I said with more reassurance than I felt. I put my pack on the dining room table and pulled out my first aid kit and grabbed a folded metal splint and started straightening and bending the malleable meshed metal into an arm splint. I covered the inside curve of the splint with gauze and laid out some tensor bandages and asked Miriam to bring her daughter to sit at the table. "What is your name?" I asked gently to the teenage girl.

"Mary," was the dopey reply.

"Well Mary, let's get your arm looked at," I said. We sat Mary down and I gently molded the mesh to fit her arm. I demonstrated to Randy how he would have to hold her arm and grab her hand as if shaking it. I gently probed the fracture to find out which way the bones were oriented. "Randy, you are going to have to hold her hand and arm and apply traction by pulling on her hand and holding her upper arm steady, then when I tell you, I want you to rotate her hand to the right to reduce the fracture." I demonstrated the maneuver on his arm. "She is going to yelp when you apply traction but do not stop pulling until I get the splint and wraps in place. She will feel much better once this is done."

We got into position and Mary only jumped a little bit when Randy's pressure was applied. I felt the bones lining up in her arm then told Randy to turn her hand a few more degrees to the right until they were perfectly aligned. I splinted the arm and wrapped the tensor bandages in place, keeping her arm in the desired position. I pulled a chemical ice pack out of my bag and squeezed and shook the contents to activate it. "Now Miriam," I said. "One hour on, one hour off for the ice pack. It will reduce the swelling and help with the pain. She is young and will heal in about six to eight weeks. Give her Ibuprofen for the pain if you have it as it is better at reducing swelling than aspirin or acetaminophen."

"Thank you so much," Miriam said thankfully. "I would not know what to do without you."

"Do you have a shotgun Miriam?" I asked pointedly.

"Yes but I don't know how to use it," she replied, looking down at the tops of her shoes.

"Go get it and I will show you." Miriam grabbed the semi-automatic trap gun from the kitchen with a box of birdshot and handed it to me. I demonstrated how to load the gun and how to operate the safety. "Now, you are loaded with birdshot. The shells are filled with gunpowder and tiny little steel pellets. It won't do much damage to anyone at the end of your driveway but close up it is pretty devastating. Do you have a neighbor or family close by that you can stay with?"

"Mary's friend lives next door and both her parents are home," she replied. "We know them through the various school and church events. Our daughters have been friends since elementary school and we have been carpooling since then."

"Good, let's go see them," I said. We went to a similar sized house and lot next door and saw a large muscled man at the side of the house chopping wood using a maul in a practiced steady stroke. He stopped when he saw us and picked up a side by side shotgun propped up next to his growing wood stack. He kept the shotgun lowered when he recognized Miriam and saw that we were armed but not brandishing weapons.

"Everything OK Miriam?" he asked as we approached.

"Oh yes," she said. "This is Mr. Robertson from down the street. He helped Mary with her arm. This is Adam, my neighbor."

"You were the guys that helped my daughter out the other day," Adam said. "I want to thank you. Care for some coffee?"

"Please," I said as we walked into his spacious, cozy, rustic kitchen placing our long guns at the door.

"Darn electricity has shut down my water. I have an old hand dug well and have been using the water in my cistern and hot water tank. I am not too sure what I'm going to do after that goes dry other than using a bucket and a string for the well. I have a camping trailer out back that we use for showers and toilet but I have to carry the water over there," Adam said. You don't see too many old hand dug wells but I noticed that the creek on my property ran past Adam's house.

Randy sprang from his seat and said, "Let's go take a look."

We walked out to his water shed behind the house and saw an old concrete cistern with a 110AC pump and pressure tank for his house. "Do you have any water pipes and a bicycle pump?" Randy asked excitedly after checking out the set up.

"Yes," said Adam. "But I don't have the ability to run the 110AC well pump. I have a solar panel set for the trailer but I don't have an inverter to hook up to the pump. My array isn't big enough."

"This keeps getting better and better," said Randy excitedly. "We are going to set up your panels and pull the DC water pump from your trailer and use it to pump water from your well into your cistern. Then you need to use a bicycle pump to blow up your pressure tank using the nipple on the top. It will only last for about twelve minutes but you can shower and use your toilet if you have a gravity septic system."

Adam smiled seeing Randy's plan in his head. "I even have an emergency car compressor for inflating car tires that runs on DC. If I pull the batteries from my truck and hook it up to my solar panels then I won't even have to pump."

A half an hour later Adam had running water in his house and could not thank us enough. Miriam and Adam's wife and daughter were in the kitchen staring in amazement as Adam demonstrated the running water. "Can you do my house?" Miriam asked.

"Do you have a shallow or deep well?" I asked.

"Deep," was her reply.

"Then no," I said. "The DC water pumps are not strong enough to lift the water from the deep wells. You would need a solar 110AC pump, large solar array and inverter to make that work."

"Maybe you and Mary could come stay here until your husband returns," offered Adam. "We don't have a lot but I'm sure if we pool our resources and labor we will be stronger together...plus we have running water," he said with a grin.

"In the land of the blind the one-eyed man is King," quipped Miriam with a smile. "Thank you guys so much. I will run home and pack up all our food and some clothes. I have been canning for a few years now as a hobby so we should be in good shape."

Adam explained that he was a logging foreman and was worried about all the strangers coming down the road and asking for help. "Some of those guys give me the creeps. That's why I always keep my shotgun nearby."

"Well Adam," I said thoughtfully. "I would suggest that you go talk to all your neighbors and drop some large trees across the road. If you stagger them you can make an Abatis so a vehicle can get through but have to slow down and do two switchbacks. It will also funnel any people to the center of the road. If you can organize your neighbors you can have a neighborhood watch to help with security. You guys are pretty exposed down here and need to cut down the avenues people can take to approach your property. A few trees across your driveway and you will have a fairly defensible position."

"How will emergency responders get to us if we partially block the road?" asked Adam.

"I don't think they are coming Adam but you do have the skills to open the road if needed with a chainsaw," I replied. "Better safe and wrong than exposed and wrong."

"Is there anything I can do for you guys?" Adam asked.

"Funny you should mention it," I replied with a smile. "I see you have a log splitter over there and know your way around a chainsaw. I'd be happy to trade say five pounds of meat and a basket of vegetables for a cord of wood. I have the trees on my property but am a danger to myself and others with a chainsaw. I also see you have a teenage daughter. We have some little ones that need babysitting and schooling for say two dozen eggs a week. How does that sound?"

"You have a deal sir," said Adam with a smile, shaking my hand sealing the deal. "I'll keep you in wood and child minding for as long and as much as you need in exchange for food. I was a little worried about the pantry if this was a long term event and you have taken a big load off my mind. Where do I need to go?"

I explained how to get to my house and told him to buzz the gate before entering. "Now Adam, my house location cannot be revealed under any circumstance to anyone or our deal is terminated. Do you understand that? Security is everything now otherwise people will kill you even for what they think you have. Take a couple of days to get settled and we will hook up then."

Randy and I walked away with a wave. "That was pretty generous of you."

"Adam seems like a good man taking Miriam and her daughter in without a thought. He is also helping secure the only road to our house which is critical. The trade was worth it, especially if Miriam is a canning machine. We are potentially going to have a lot of fresh produce that we are going to have to preserve to get through the winter," I explained while Randy and I walked back to my homestead.

Our new extended family spent the next two weeks getting the homestead ready for the future. We planted the entire field with winter wheat and corn, sowing the seeds by hand into the loose tilled earth. The chicken coop was expanded using lumber I had hand salvaged from various surplus lumber supplies I had left over from my home building projects. We fenced it using the extra chicken wire Cindy had brought from the feed store in her truck digging the wire into the ground and burying it in a two-foot trench so predators could not dig under the wire into the coop. We also built nesting beds for the chickens to lay their eggs and rigged the coop with heat lamps to keep the chickens warm in the winter. We installed the wood burning stove and flue outside on the patio for the remainder of the summer and fall, preplanning a spot just inside the house to keep us warm in the winter. We constructed a greenhouse on the former upper lawn in an area that had the best southern sun exposure using more lumber and extra windows I had from jobsites. We also wrapped any other areas of the greenhouse with clear rolled plastic I had. We worked hard from dawn until dusk and were bone weary tired by the end of the day. Adam, true to his word, put up ten chords of wood and helped secure our driveway by dropping a few well-placed trees. Amy, our neighbor at the end of the driveway, came over every day with her two kids, a girl who was eight and a son that was six. Amy is a proud single mother and refused the offer to move in with us but was there daily to help with our projects and ate her meals with us. Randy and I set out tripwires on all approaches to the property rigged with noisemakers and flares and he was a godsend with his mechanical abilities, setting up a full irrigation system for our crops by digging up and repurposing our lawn sprinkler system, creating drip tubes for our rows of plants. We constructed a reinforced bunker on the field side of the driveway behind a cedar tree that we had left to block the view of the house from the gate and camouflaged the bunker. I knew the most likely avenue of attack would be down the driveway. We also rigged up a few surprises for any attackers trying to attack our house from this vector. He installed two ingenious hot water coil syphons piped from our stove, one for the house domestic water supply and one copper loop that kept our greenhouse warm using the copper and hot water as a radiator. He explained that a hot water syphon could take cold water from the bottom of our tanks at the drain port, circulate the water through a copper coil in the firebox and add the now near boiling water up to the top of our hot water tanks teeing into the cold water tie in. Randy also assembled a ram pump for the creek to get Amy's house water stored in a tote we set up on a wood platform in a tree and another one for our house to fill two five hundred gallon water totes for irrigation to keep the solar pump from working too hard. We had to dam off a portion of the creek to create a pool of water to provide us with a steady head of water pressure and installed the drive line with a screen to stop creek debris from jamming up the pumps. The creek is about 1000 feet from out water totes but only had an elevation change of 10 feet. Fortunately we had enough PEX tubing to make the run instead of using garden hose. The rubber garden hoses would have absorbed too much pressure to make the distance providing too much water friction. With Adam's selective logging we were able to manhandle our large fifth wheel with our tractor so it was hidden in our adjoining five acres. We dug a large hole in the ground and built an insulated rooftop for our generator to shield it from noise and after many failed attempts managed to get it to work on wood gas. We built a gasifier by placing a sealed ammo box for the chipped wood fuel into our stove fire box. We installed a baffle in the ammo box to keep the wood gas fuel out of a sealed plumbing fitting coming out of the ammo box. After many failed attempts we learned we had to install a fan in the wood stove to get the fire to burn hotter and a condenser to cool the wood gas before it entered the generator air intake. We also learned to install pipe dirt legs on the bottom of the condenser grille to capture the oily substance that was gumming up the pipes. The gasifier wood gas to generator connection needed an air mixer valve to add oxygen to the wood gas to achieve combustion. It took us many failed attempts to get the system working properly after ironing out all the kinks in the system. I had researched online and in multiple prepper forums where to purchase a readymade gasifier but most of the companies making them all went out of business for lack of sales. There are only so many off grid preppers out there and using loud generators to make electricity is not high on their priorities with solar panel arrays and micro hydro generators becoming less expensive due to government and utility subsidies available in the marketplace. Randy and I were working on setting up a canning station and wood smoker when the dogs started barking and took off like a shot down the driveway. I was very pleased to see the little ones and Jacob bolt for the house and the adults running swiftly to the rally point with long guns in hand. After meeting the group at the rally point, I cautiously worked my way down the woods next to the driveway under the cover of my extended family. I saw Mr. Jones and some of the people from the neighborhood at the end of my driveway behind the gate. I cautiously approached the group but saw they were unarmed.

"Can I help you?" I asked. "Did you not see the private property sign as you came down the gravel road?"

"Um, yes," stammered Mr. Jones. "But we are here on a matter of some importance. You see, I am the President of the homeowner's association and at our scheduled meeting last night we took a vote and decided that all the homes in the neighborhood needed to pool our resources in these troubling times. We decided that all food needed to be brought to the community and shared equally amongst all the people based on a pro rata share. Everything needs to be surrendered immediately and hoarding is not permitted."

"I see," I replied with condescending malice. "Did any of you help me plant my field? Did any of you offer to trade me for food? Are any of you helping secure and defend the neighborhood? Do you expect me to just give up what is mine? Because if so I can assure you we have both the will and the capability to defend what is ours and any person who comes to this gate uninvited in the future will summarily be shot; just so we are clear."

"You can't threaten me," blustered Mr. Jones, puffing out his chest. "I'll go see the sheriff and have you arrested. I am the President of the HOA."

I laughed out loud as he turned on his heel and stormed off in a huff. I noticed that his posse were still standing around shaking their heads in disdain as he stomped up my gravel path. I walked up to my gate and addressed the crowd. "If any of you want to work in producing, processing or defending food then I will either help you or help you help yourselves. We are a community of people that are stronger together but this is not communism, there are no free rides."

The group of remaining people huddled together in a conference and finally a consensus was arrived at with all the heads bobbing up and down. A good looking haggard blond lady came forward. "We just disbanded the homeowner's association. What should we do next?"

"Well," I replied. "Anyone is welcome to come work in our field at a rate of one meal per half day. Children under the age of eight can come to our school and receive two meals for the day. Kids over the age of eight can join our foraging parties we will set up. Any person who serves four hours of security at Adam's blockade at the bottom of the hill or prepares meals will receive a meal. I will show any of you who want to learn how to hunt, forage or grow food, how to do so and will supply seeds to grow into food. We will also set up a trading post at the blockade for people outside the community to trade with ours. For those of you with special skills we can trade as needed. The cul-de-sac will be the place for community meals. We are living in a barter economy and your work is your value to your family and the neighborhood."

"Sounds reasonable to me," said the blond lady. "My husband is a doctor who is still working at the hospital. We have two teenagers, a boy of fifteen and a girl who is fourteen. My eighty-year-old mother in law Ginny is staying with us. What can she do?"

"Your mother in law might just be our most valuable asset," I lectured looking at the assembled group. "She is a pre-war depression era child. She will know everything there is to know about canning, gardening, sewing, composting and cooking on a wood stove. People from that era know what it is like to have been hungry and cold. They lived before the advent of supermarkets and fast food. I would suggest your mother in law can give classes to all the neighborhood ladies, share recipes and lessons in homesteading. I'll bet she even knows how to make things like soap. We will get through this together but only if we work together. I will be up in the cul-de-sac tomorrow morning and we will figure out how to get everyone pulling together."

"Wow!" one of the men said. "We can't thank you enough. When Mr. Jones told us to bring all our food over to his garage I was thinking; what food?"

"There are always people who will choose to take from others by legal means," I explained. "They are called politicians. Where else can you take money from people in the form of taxes and spend that money on buying votes and campaign contributions for yourself. Hell, they can even borrow additional money and go into debt to buy your vote with your own future earnings. Crazy system and look how that worked out for them. I'm sure they are all sitting in hardened bunkers with ready-made meals that we bought for them while the people, whose money paid for these meals and accommodations, starve."

The procession moved up the driveway and were passed by two people coming in the opposite direction. It was my father in law Marcus and his wife Joy riding their mountain bikes. Avery would be so happy. I gave them a hug as I opened the gate for them.

"How goes the road?" I asked. As we came into view of the house, I heard the unmistakable "Grandpa!" shriek from Avery as she came running down the driveway to jump into her grandfather's arms.

He laughed. "The migration has begun down HWY 16," he said. "There are masses of people trying to get out of the City into the country thinking that is where the food is. We took the backroads in and those are pretty quiet. A few people took a try for the bikes but we were faster and a couple of booms from old Betty, my carriage gun, sent them scattering. It's a mess out there but we at least saw some of the old purse seiners coming out and going in."

"Good," I said. "Gig Harbor is an old fishing village and those old coots know how to catch a lot of fish to keep people fed. I hope they are getting their shit together and blocking the bridges and blockading the inlets and harbor entrances. It won't be long before the Tacoma masses just across the bridges to the East run out of food and start looking our way."

Belle's parents were both outdoors people who liked to camp and fish. They would be an asset to our homestead and little Avery absolutely adores them. We set them up in the guest bedroom and had a group meeting.

"It looks like our neighborhood finally wants to come into the fold," I said. "They just needed a small dose of reality to see the error of their ways. The good news is we might have a doctor in the community when he makes it back from the hospital. The garden is doing well and the crops will have some more hands in the morning to help with weeding and tending the harvest."

"You mean except for those darn rabbits and deer that keep eating it?" asked Randy.

I laughed. "You mean they have fallen for the bait? Jacob?"

"Yes sir," he said with confidence. "I'm on it."

"Marcus?" I asked looking in his direction with a raised eyebrow. "Can you help Jacob make a bunch of snares and help Jacob and Randy tonight with the watch? Randy and I will build a hutch for the ones that make it."

"No problem," said Marcus. "Shooter?" he asked, already understanding my intention.

"Just watch," I smiled and gave him a wink.

Randy looked at us with confusion on his round face.

"Randy," I explained. "Jacob is going to shoot the deer that come by tonight for their dinner with his suppressed rifle. You and Marcus are going to process any deer Jacob manages to bring down. Fortunately the dogs don't bark at deer. Marcus and Jacob are going to make rabbit snares out of picture wire and set them out. The snares don't always kill the trapped rabbits so we will capture any live ones and put them in a pen. I'm sure you've heard the term "going at it like bunnies?" Well bunnies reproduce quickly and grow meat at a rapid rate. We will set up a large dog pen enclosure and put the live ones in the pen. We only need to keep moving the pen over fresh vegetation and bunnies will do what bunnies do best. Marcus, please make a whole bunch of extra snares and a couple of sets of figure four sticks and we will take Jacob with us tomorrow to get the community teens working at trapping rabbits and limb rats. Joy, if you can please come with us and show the ladies what edibles can be harvested from the woods while Randy and I get the cul-de-sac people set up with a garden plot, irrigation and a greenhouse."

"Won't that put a strain on our food supply helping those people?" asked Randy demurely.

"Not if Jacob can shoot straight, rabbits stay dumb and the community pulls together to get some seed in the ground. It is a short term cost in exchange for a long term food and security solution," I explained. "Winter will be tough but thanks to Cindy and the coop, the four acres of food we have in the ground and everyone working together we will prevail. We will probably have a few farm hands tomorrow. Cindy and Amy, I really need you two to watch them carefully. Let me know if any of them decide to take a walk around to check things out. Under no circumstance do we talk about food, ourselves, our resources or let anyone in the house. We will spend the afternoon digging an outhouse for the field help. I think they are all harmless but we need to be safe. Our evening watches will be augmented to three people with one on the roof, one on the patio and a roving walking patrol. You all have your whistles and blow them if anything seems out of place. Cindy, please make sure the field hands rake out the perimeter soil we left around the planting so we can see footprints if anyone has been nosing about. I'm pretty sure the dogs would pick up on it but they will grow accustomed to the strangers and might not bark."

We all sat down to a good dinner of steak, potatoes and green beans. My wife had even made an apple pie with ice cream for the kids. After the kids went to bed, we enjoyed a bottle of wine and played cards. We had put up black out curtains over the dining room area and after checking outside for light leakage I walked Amy and her kids to their home. Finally I had a shower and joined my wife in bed.

"Are we doing the right thing?" she asked. My wife always had a bit of bleeding heart liberalism in her. She always tuned out politics, feeling her voice and vote were ineffective and chose to live in her "bubble" of unicorns, rainbows and real housewives of lord knows where.

"With what?" I asked.

"Not giving the neighbors food?" she said. "We always talk about doing more charity work and giving to the needy."

"Honey," I said frankly. "If we just gave them food then they would keep coming back for more. The Bible says give a man a fish and feed him for a day, teach a man to fish and feed him for his life. I'm sure that is a parable of some kind referring to teaching them God's love but we need to teach these people how to provide for themselves. I'll make sure that anyone who works hard doesn't starve and those that can't provide for themselves are taken care of but I do not have the time for idiots like Jones that feel entitled to a free hand out. They all had an equal opportunity to invest in their futures but spent their money on frivolous material goods."

"You are right," she said after thinking about it for a few seconds. "I am so happy you did not cave when I said you were spending too much on your preparations but I am so glad you did taking care of me, Avery, my family and now our expanded family."

"How happy?" I asked in a husky tone.

"I'll show you if you promise not to wake up the entire house," she said with a smile.

CHAPTER 3

We woke up the next morning to coffee and a large breakfast. I knew it would be another beautiful day with clear sunny skies just by the smell in the air. I stepped out onto the back patio and was glad to see two dressed deer hanging from gambrels over by the garage. I walked out and inspected the kills and saw two perfect heart-lung bullet holes, one in each of them. I saw Randy and he came over seeing me inspecting the deer.

"Never seen anything like it," he said with awe in his voice. "By the time I was going to whisper there's a deer, I already heard two pfft pffts next to me and both deer just wobbled and fell over. The kid just turned and looked at me, smiled a shit eating grin, and said "Well Mr. Randy, I shot them, you need to hang, gut and skin them." I looked at Marcus and he laughed at me too. Those two showed me how to hang and gut the deer, showing me on one while I had to do the other. I was hacking away with my knife when they took mercy on me and showed me how to sharpen my knife with a stone; it was much easier after that. Then they went around the property and picked up six rabbits and put the two live ones in the pen and showed me how to skin and butcher the other four. It is effing Davey Crocket and Daniel Boone you have living here. I am sure glad they are on our side."

I went over to the hung deer, took out my knife and removed two quarters from the carcasses. I wrapped the two quarters in a piece of plastic and added two of the dressed rabbits to the makeshift bag. I then went to the garden and pulled twenty carrots and dug up two onions and ten potatoes putting them in a basket. Marcus, Randy, Joy, Jacob and I loaded up the tractor with a water tote and a ram pump and set off for the cul-de-sac. There were thirty people in the street when we came driving up, ranging in ages from five to eighty. I grouped them by age group. "OK, everyone between the ages of eight and fifteen please come over here with Jacob." Six kids went to stand in a group with Jacob. "Under the age of eight please go with Joy." Four little ones came forward shyly. That left eighteen adults. "OK, who wants to help Grandma Ginny with lunch and foraging, work in the fields, join Adam for security or organize a scrounge party?" I asked. People began shuffling about. Six men signed up for farm work. Four with handguns and hunting rifles headed for the road blocks to join Adam's crew, four ladies joined Grandma Ginny and four wanted to scrounge. I gave Ginny's group the basket and plastic wrapped meat. One of them opened the plastic and held it away from her with a look of disgust on her face.

"What is this and what the hell do we do with it?" she asked slightly aghast.

Grandma Ginny came over, looked inside the plastic and said, "Ohhh, I have a great recipe for rabbit and venison stew. OK ladies, no dawdling. Get those two sawhorses over there set up by the fire pit with a piece of plywood across it. Carolyn, go get that large pot you use for the church spaghetti night and the big plastic cutting boards. Mindy, get that fire pit going, we'll have to get the stones around the fire rearranged to set the pot on. Angela, get down to the creek and keep bringing buckets of water until I tell you to stop." Ginny turned and gave me a wink. "I'll get these soccer moms whipped into shape in no time and really give them something to twitter about. I remember when a twitter was the slow kid in school."

I knew I had Ginny pegged right. "OK teens and tweens. Marcus and Jacob over here will show you how to trap animals." One of the fifteen-year-olds went up to Jacob, looking at his rifle. "Cool," he said. "Let me see that kid." Walking toward Jacob. Jacob stepped back, drew his Sig and pointed it at the teen with his finger off the trigger. "Step away!" Jacob ordered in a loud voice. The teen stopped in his tracks with his eyes wide and a look of terror in his now ghost white face.

Jacob announced. "This is my rifle, it is not a toy. If your parents, Mr. Robertson and I say it is OK then I will teach you how to use it properly but until then it is for both my and your protection. Do you understand?"

The teen was still staring at Jacob in shocked silence, knees trembling forcibly. I broke the tension by walking up to the frightened teen. "What's your name?" I asked.

"Michael," was the quiet reply with his eyes not leaving Jacob's pistol, staring at it like two lasers.

"Well Michael," I said putting my arm around his shoulders. "You just learned a life lesson. Jacob here is a crack shot, the best I've actually ever seen. I suggest you listen exactly to what he has to say and you might just live. He did shoot and trap the lunch that you will be eating today."

Marcus and Jacob took the now wild-eyed teens in tow and started showing them how to construct and set lures and traps for small animals. Marcus already had them finding, cutting, notching and sharpening sticks to set up figure four traps.

"OK," I announced to the remaining group of four. "That leaves the scroungers. Rule number one is you guys will only scrounge from abandoned cars and places. If I hear of a single theft I will shoot you myself. Top trade items will be prescription drugs, gas, diesel, garden tools, ammunition, pre-1965 silver coins, alcohol and food I imagine you would like to keep for yourself. Anything else that you find we can barter for or you can sell at the trading station we will be setting up down the street. Questions?"

"What is each item worth?" one of them tentatively asked.

"That entirely depends on supply and demand," I replied. "Right now I need diesel, gas and garden tools. Our medium of exchange will be ammunition or eggs. I am not sure how much silver is in circulation but we can work that out in the future. Right now, five gallons of gas or diesel is worth ten rounds of ammunition or two eggs. Each shovel or rake is worth one egg or five rounds. The community meals you can work out with the ladies in the kitchen. Remember that safety is the most important thing. Two of you can work while the other two provide over watch protection. The easiest way to siphon gas is to spike the tank but I'm sure Randy over here can rig you up something faster and easier. Wood smoke, light, garbage and trampled grass are pretty tell-tale signs that a place is occupied. You will also probably learn to tell all the different smells that will signal if a place is occupied or not. DO NOT STEAL under any circumstances."

"OK, we have this," replied one of them without too much confidence. "Is there any way we can get an advance on today's gas and diesel? We only have 10 rounds of 9 MM between us and you did say safety is first."

I laughed and pulled out my two spare Glock clips from my belt. I counted out the thirty rounds of hollow point defense rounds. "OK, you owe me fifteen gallons tonight and let me know what you guys run into out there. Stay off the main roads, scrounging involves as much reconnaissance as looting."

After everyone had left, except Randy and me, Ginny walked over and gave me a hug. There was some steel in her arms. "You are doing right by these people Mr. Robertson. They don't appreciate it now but I am sure they will come winter. It brings back fond memories of times with my parents learning all these lost arts. They are all good people. They won't let you down."

"Please Ginny," I said in reproach. "My name is James. You are a remarkable woman and between the two of us I'm sure we will pull through. Is there anything you need?"

"No," she replied. "I have a little heart arrhythmia but I have a few months' supply of medication. Other than that, I am as fit as a fiddle."

"Well," I said, "We will get that to the top of the scrounge list then. Do you know who owns the house across the street here?" I asked, pointing at a house with a lush expansive lawn area and surrounding garden.

Ginny looked over at me with a smile. "That is Angela's house. The yard crew is here every week with the reel movers. I've even seen her husband, who is now incidentally one of your new field hands, putting golf balls on it from time to time. They plug and top dress it every year and fertilize twice a year. I bet that would make the finest garden in the area. Angela!" she yelled with a strong set of lungs. "We need to see you for a minute."

Angela came running over while Randy was already at the creek setting up the ram pump drive pipe and water supply pipe. Ginny put her arm around Angela's shoulders and pointed at her lawn. "I want you to imagine that beautiful green lawn as a beautiful garden chock full of fresh vegetables ready to eat. Can you picture it?"

Angela laughed. "I would trade it in a second. My husband loves that lawn but he would love food even more right about now."

Ginny gave me a nod as I hopped on and started up the tractor and began tilling Angela's lawn. It was easy tilling as the topsoil was very deep and the grass very fine. It only took an hour to till an acre sized garden. Randy already had the tote set up that was already filling with water and pointed at the irrigation lines. I shook my head so we dropped off a one acre tub of heirloom seeds I had previously bought online, loaded up the tractor and were heading back to the homestead when Adam rode up on a bike.

"How are you?" he asked with a wave. He had outfitted his bike with a scabbard to hold his shotgun and a handlebar rest if he needed to aim while pedaling.

"Fantastic!" I replied.

"Thanks for the extra security," he said. "I don't have to feed them, do I?"

"No," I replied with a chuckle. "The cul-de-sac neighborhood will take care of it. But I'm sure the group up here needs some fire wood and will trade. Any action at the road block?"

"No," said Adam. Just then we heard a gunshot from down the street. I unslung my rifle and Randy, Adam and I proceeded cautiously to the roadblock. There were three guards behind the log barrier with their rifles trained down the street to the East while the fourth was watching the other direction in case it was a diversionary attack.

"Report!" said Adam walking up to one of the guards.

One of the new guards turned to us and said, "Two riders were approaching. We yelled at them to stop but they kept coming. One of them had a handgun pointed toward the barricade so I fired a warning shot. They both fell off their bikes and hightailed it in the other direction."

"Good job," I said. "Next time no warning shot. Let's put a sign down the road so people can read it saying "Walkers only, proceed with your hands outstretched or you will be fired upon" or stick a few white flags down there that people can wave. Our neighborhood is now closed. Maybe we can also rig up a bell down here for you guys. One ring means people approaching. Three rings means shots fired and continuous rings means the shit has hit the fan and help is needed right now."

I saw Miriam at the end of Adam's driveway toting her shotgun, looking toward the barricade. She waved and said Mary's arm was feeling much better and thanked me for the help. I walked with Adam to the bottom of my street.

"How are you holding up?" I asked him.

"We are doing OK," he replied with confidence. "I took a couple of deer a few days ago, the water works and we have a black barrel on the roof making hot water. Things could be a lot worse but winter is coming. The migration seems to have ended but food is on everyone's mind and there are plenty of people out looking for it. There is a group of escaped convicts from the women's prison holed up in Kopachuck State Park and we seem to be on the direct path between there and the City. We have heard rumors of a gang that took over the Rosedale gardens and all the plants there. We also see a lot of people with fishing poles heading down to Wollocet Bay. We have heard of a group of bikers up in Key Penninsula that are consolidating everything west of the spit and are actually forcing anyone who won't work for them or join their army to cross the spit out of town. They have formed chain gangs for all the able bodies to work the farms up there and all of the bars up in Key Peninsula are now brothels where they pimp out anyone wanting to work there. There is also a group up by the grange that has blocked the main road to the City from Fox Island that is demanding tolls from anyone using the road."

"If you need anything Adam, please don't hesitate to ask," I told him. "I always need more wood and we are looking at clearing some of Amy's five acres to plant in the spring."

"I'll keep that in mind," said Adam. "I am not looking for charity but really appreciate you taking care of the girls up at your school and looking out for the neighborhood. We would be in deep trouble if it was everyone for themselves like all the other neighborhoods we are hearing about are doing."

I knew it would only be a matter of time before people start to get more desperate as their pantries run dry and realize there is no more food to be had. It is now almost three weeks and the reality of the situation might finally be hitting home.

"We are eventually going to have to start reaching out to our adjoining neighborhoods to see if any of them are organized. It looks like there are two other barricades on this street, one from the toll takers and the other from the State Park women. Right now they are helping keep us safe and that is our priority even if they could be potential future problems. Hey, is that the scrounge team I see down by your place?" I asked, identifying the group of four who I trade gas with.

"Well yes," Adam replied with a smile. "I trade hot showers for the first shot at any loot they bring in. We compare notes on safety concerns while my wife and Miriam have been known to launder their clothes for a small fee. The scroungers say about fifty percent of the houses in a five mile radius are empty. They are staying safe. They are calling their point man "Lucky Lew," he is their door knocker. He has managed to only take one shell of birdshot in his ass that he had patched up by a nurse up the street. They started with a wheelbarrow but now have a couple of four wheelers and flatbeds that they haul their loot in. They have been asking about opening safes but they haven't found a safe cracker yet. They can open the small three by three Costco fire safes with a metal wedge and sledgehammer but the gun safes are beyond their skill. They say the worst problem is a pack of feral dogs that is forming up by Artondale Elementary school. It seems a lot of people just let their dogs go when they ran out of dog food. We shoot every dog we see down here at the barricade and add them to the forever soup pot we keep running down here for the guards, figuring it is the best for everyone long term. If these dogs start getting the taste for people then we could have a big problem since there used to be as many dogs as people around here. Your friend Mr. Jones was found stabbed and tortured down by the grange. There have been some people in the area that have asked to join our neighborhood and one of our guards that signed on lives three blocks outside the barricade, he works the day shift for a meal but has to get back home to keep it safe in the evening. What do you think about moving the abatis down?"

"I don't see an issue with it," I replied looking at the tactical situation. "But you will have to protect two fronts which will take twice as many guards as you currently have and there is the potential to be protecting a bunch of people that are not contributing to their own defense. We don't want to get into the "protection racket" where we tax people in exchange for security. Why don't we look at letting people move into any empty houses that we currently have? It is kind of like a job interview. If people like your guard and the nurse that patched up Lew want to join the neighborhood and they have skills we need then they can move into places like Communist Jones' old house."

"Sounds good to me," said Adam thinking about who would be an asset. "Who is the decider on neighborhood applications?"

"Send them to Ginny," I laughed. "That will set them far straighter than I could. That old bird could stop on a nickel and pick up a dime."

Randy and I headed home. All this walking and hard work has definitely redirected the flow of gravity from my pony keg belly to my flat chest. We saw Jacob talking to Ginny at the cul-de-sac along with the foragers doing their daily drop off.

"How goes it Jacob?" I asked cheerily.

"Well sir, as I was telling Mrs. Ginny here, the trap line is being raided so the take is not as strong as it was," Jacob said. "But the fruit trees are all in season and the berries are starting to come in."

"Do you think the raiders are of the two legged or four legged variety?" I asked, hoping for the latter but knowing it was only a matter of time before people started raiding our traps.

"The tracks indicate coyote or dog sir. There are five or six black bears that I have seen tracks for, a couple of foxes and quite a few deer. I am thinking four legged because our tree limb rat lines are untouched. I am trying to figure out how to guard the traps but some of the teens are too noisy, don't understand wind direction and scare all the game away even though the rabbit population in these woods is astronomical," said Jacob pensively.

"OK," I replied, thinking the problem through and figuring the likely culprits. "I hate to do it but let's pull three quarters of the snare lines and place them by the victory gardens. Take Marcus and set up the conibear traps, large gauge snares and some big figure four stick traps on the other small game snares. We are going to have to thin the predator herd out there. Do you have any teens in your crew that can keep their mouths shut, shoot straight and do what they are told?"

"Um, um," stammered Jacob with his eyes darting around shyly. "Ginny's thirteen-year-old granddaughter is actually the best of the bunch by far, sir. She learns quickly, doesn't get queasy around the animal killing and processing and is like Annie Oakley with a suppressed .22."

"I noticed she isn't bad looking either," I observed while watching Jacob blush to the roots of his short cut hair and avoid eye contact with Ginny and I. "There are rumors of a feral dog pack about five miles from here and these woods are crawling with coyotes. You guys are going to end up with a few golden doodles in your traps. A dog is almost anatomically identical to a coyote so other than the three of us here, Marcus and the lovely Alisha, nobody is to know that we are trapping dogs. Stay in a group of three and get up a tree if a large pack of dogs is coming your way."

Ginny turned and gave Jacob a smack upside the head. "And that's just so you remember to keep my "lovely" granddaughter safe young man. Keep your eyes open for danger and not on her backside or so help me you'll end up in my pot. Understand?"

"Yes ma'am," Jacob said as he turned to give his crew their instructions.

Ginny turned to me and said quietly, "That might be the most polite, well mannered, capable young man I've ever met. I am going to have to have a few words with Alisha."

"Don't go planning the wedding just yet," I laughed at Ginny. "He is only thirteen."

"James," she said grimly. "I think you will find that these times will mimic those of the Second World War when fourteen and fifteen became the new nineteen and twenty. There is already a lot of misery out there and it will only get worse come winter when the great starvation sets in. Alisha is already thirteen and turning fourteen by the end of the year. If she is as smitten with him as he seems to be with her then "the talk" is coming sooner than you think. Now get on your way, I have things to do. And find me some swine and some corn. The darn swill is going to the compost heap instead of to some pigs."

She turned to her soccer mom brigade and continued her soap making and hide tanning session. There had been a huge turnaround in the group as they all had their hair tied up at the back of their heads in buns and were all wearing aprons. Amazing how fewer showers and doing laundry by hand changed one's perspective quickly. It was far more convenient keeping your hair out of your work and cleaning an apron than washing your hair in the solar shower and cleaning an entire change of clothes. I don't think many of them knew that most people in the pre-war era only bathed on Sundays, with each member of the family reusing the same bath water and only had two or three changes of clothes. The community had constructed a set of three solar showers behind plastic shower curtains and large kettles set up as a communal laundry. They had also set up a slew of picnic benches for community meals with pop up tent shelters for shade. Our neighborhood had only lost three households since "the event": Mr. Jones, Mr. Clancy, a diabetic and Mr. King, an elderly gentleman with a pacemaker that had shorted out during the EMP.

I headed back to the homestead and started working on digging out the pressure canner and water bath canner from my garage. I had picked up the equipment from the local goodwill which was rife with them and had been amassing mason jars over the last few years at local garage sales. I was by no means an expert and didn't have any of the large crock pots I knew people used for pickling and preparing their produce for canning; I would have to ask Ginny and Miriam for some pointers since we always donated our unused produce at the end of the season to our local food bank. I did have a large supply of canning salt and spices but knew that canning produce was one thing but having it taste good and fresh in the future would be an asset. I set up an area for slicing and dicing the produce using a piece of butcher block countertop I had salvaged from a remodel I had done. My wife always accused me of being a pack rat but I knew the butcher block cutting board didn't take up much space and I always used it for putting my large plastic deer processing plastic board on for butchering meat. I had a Coleman camping stove for the pressure canner and would use our camping barbeque for the water bath canner. I also had an air compressor vacuum lid sealer for produce we would use in the next 30 days. I knew the canning would be hard hot work so I set up the station on the North shaded side of the house for the two to three week post-harvest time frame window that would be afforded us. I was working on setting up the station when my radio in the workshop suddenly crackled to life. I had it tuned to the distress channel but it had remained silent until now.

"XMJ 657, calling XMJ 657, this is XLK 988. I repeat this is XLK 988 calling XMJ 657," it squawked. I had bought an old antique ham radio a few years back at an estate sale. It had old school vacuum tubes in it and on a lark I had taken a test and received a ham radio license the previous year. XMJ 657 was my FCC license number so whoever was on the radio was calling me.

"This is XMJ 657, I read you five by five," I said into the handset.

"Give me that," I heard a gruff voice in the background say. "Robertson, is that you? It's Stutz over here in Arletta."

I heard in the background a voice saying, "…Mr. Stutz, you have to say "over" when you are done speaking and release the handset lever."

"…who the hell is "over"? Am I not talking to Robertson on this thing?"

"…sir, just release the little lever and say "over," I know it is stupid but only one person can talk at a time on one of these radios and saying over lets the other party know you are done speaking."

"…Well Excuse me! Robertson, it's Stutz; are you there, OVER?"

"I'm here Mr. Stutz, what is your status; Over?" I replied with a big grin on my face, picturing Mr. Stutz badgering his radio operator.

"It is looking like a monkey fucking a football out there but we are getting on. How about you...?" There was dead air for a few seconds until "OVER" came across the air. I laughed.

"We are getting by, Cindy and the kids are doing well. I heard there are a few pests out in your neck of the woods, over," I said.

"That's what I want to talk to you about other than how Cindy and the kids were doing, how about a face to face at the little 'un's AE at noon tomorrow? Over," said Mr. Stutz.

"Roger that, over," I replied.

"Who the hell is Roger? Over," said Mr. Stutz.

"Um, it means I read you loud and clear Mr. Stutz. Over," I replied with a chuckle.

"Then say that you wisenheimer, tomorrow noon AE. Be there. Over," he said gruffly.

"Yes sir, this is XJM 657, over and out," I said.

"Out where? Over," I heard over the speaker. "Oh...this is XLK 988 over and out you two jackasses, it's not like there is an FCC anymore to take your licenses away."

I walked outside laughing to myself and had just started setting up the rest of the trestles when I heard a lot of dogs barking and one in obvious distress coming from the woods behind my house where Mr. and Mrs. Black live. They were Bouvier dog breeders and I had met them at a few dog shows. Mr. Black occasionally played the bagpipes on the weekend and I knew they kept a few horses on their pasture acreage behind me. I grabbed Randy and shouldered my rifle to go see what the fuss was about. I went to the small section of fence at the corner of my property and peered over cautiously. Mr. Black had a machete in his hand and had taken down one of his dogs in his yard. The others in a chain link kennel were going crazy at the sight and sound of the dying dog at Mr. Black's feet.

"Hello Mr. Black," I yelled over the noise. He turned and came over to the fence. "Everything OK?" I asked.

"Yes," he replied sadly. Mr. Black was in his mid-sixties with the weathered look of someone who had worked outside his entire life. "We have six dogs and we have run out of dog food for them. I couldn't just turn them loose to fend for themselves so we are slaughtering all but two of them to help secure the property. The horses will have to be next since we are running out of food and it is hard to keep them out of the garden I planted."

"I tell you what Mr. Black," I said thinking quickly. "How about I loan you my suppressed 9MM handgun so your remaining dogs don't hear the whimpering and we look at doing a trade for the horses? I admire you doing the right thing with your dogs but would hate to see the horses needlessly slaughtered. Are they broke?"

"Yes," he replied. "The horses were my daughter's show horses and they are fine animals but I don't have enough fencing and neither my wife nor I ride. I'm not sure how I'll preserve all that meat but right now they are just a nuisance."

"I'll tell you what," I said. "I have a bunch of fencing and my crew over here will put it up around your garden. If you let the horses graze on your pasture, and provide the tack and barn space then I will buy them from you."

"You can't eat money," was his reply.

"I was thinking of replacing them pound for pound for food," I said. "Gas and diesel will eventually all go bad and other than pedal power, horses will become the next mode of transportation and field work. My wife can ride but we can always slaughter them later if it doesn't work out. I can also replace the dog meat for you if you want to trade. I know those dogs were your wife's hard work and dedication and if you prefer I can replace them with some feral dogs or coyotes we are trapping."

"Oh my goodness," he said, brightening up considerably. "That would be much appreciated. My wife is pretty distraught at the idea of eating her own dogs and our daughter's horses but you have to do the right thing and survive."

"No problem Mr. Black," I replied, shaking his proffered hand. "I'll bring the fence builders over now, install a gate here and drop off the food here as well. If it is OK I would like to cross your property from time to time since it saves a ten mile trip to go around. I will leave a note with the food of when I intend to cross or ring a bell in an emergency. That way you won't shoot me by mistake."

"Do you have any extra ammunition by chance?" he asked. "I would have shot the dogs but I am running low on ammunition."

"I can probably hook you up," I replied. "We are trading one shell per pound of meat, you seem to now have around a 2,000 pound credit with me. What do you need?"

"How about two boxes of 12 gauge buckshot, 50 rounds of .30-06 and 50 rounds of .45?" he asked.

"No problem," I replied. "Let me get you that now. I am heading to Arletta tomorrow at 9AM so please don't shoot me with your new rounds."

I went back to the shop and grabbed the ammunition Mr. Black requested and wrapped a half of deer that Randy had shot the previous night on watch in brown paper and left them at the small exposed fence section between our properties. Fortunately Mr. Black was keeping two of his dogs since they and the ammunition I was providing would keep our "Back door" more secure. I knew the conibear traps Marcus, Jacob and Alisha were putting out would quickly produce the replacement meat for the Blacks. I took a hard look at our food stores. We were in good shape before the EMP "day" having around three years of non-perishable and dried food on hand. I had been using any consulting fees and reimbursement checks I had received in the last three years to build our stores. Once a month I would go to the bulk discount cash and carry or Costco and load up on food staples like rice, beans, sugar, wheat berries, pasta and sealing them in mylar bags, adding oxygen scrubbers or dry ice into food grade five gallon buckets. I had also bought a one year program from both Wise and Mountain House. My food storage was designed for just the three of us so with ten of us eating out of our stores and the supplemental food we were sending Ginny and people like Adam we were only down around 15 percent due to our garden and hunting. It was pretty simple math to work out the daily caloric intake versus what we had stored and growing in the field. We would have a surplus through the winter but after accounting for the entire neighborhood we would be at a net deficit until the chickens came on line. I had buried half of the food grade buckets of our stores by the 5th wheel backup post. That evening after we had showered and sat down for a family meal of deer stew and vegetables, I asked about the school and how everyone was doing. My wife reported that the teens running the school were doing well with the little ones spending half the day on the three R's and the afternoons working on the farm. The kids were in charge of the chicken coop and rabbit hutch as well as picking weeds from the fields and greenhouse and feeding them to their "bunnies." The school was set up in our two car garage so I would have to set up a wood stove for the winter. We said goodnight early since every morning came quickly and there was always more to do. It was around four AM when the alarm was sounded and I could hear gunfire from my rooftop. It sounded like all hell was breaking loose as I scrambled to put on my bulletproof vest that one of the scroungers had traded to me, my load kit and boots. My rifle was at my bedside and I had it at the ready and was heading to the rally point. We had gunfire incoming from the gate and driveway but most of it was concentrated on the roof. Randy was up there and used the security alarm communication box we had rigged up there.

"There are six coming up the drive," he said rapidly into the box with deep breaths. "I'm hit in the leg and leaking but it doesn't seem bad."

I looked out a window and saw muzzle flashes coming from the tree line next to the driveway. I looked at my wife, father in law Marcus, Joy and Cindy. "OK," I said looking at each of them. "I need covering fire at those flashes. Marcus and I will flank right like we planned. Keep firing to keep their heads down. Marcus, don't engage until I give the signal. Once you hear Bessy fire then hit the lights Belle. Clear?" Everyone nodded. "Ok, let's go on three."

The ladies opened up on the attackers while Marcus and I sprinted for the few trees and emplacement I had built on the left, field side of the driveway. I had my night vision monocular on and could see four of the six shooters clearly outlined behind trees firing at the house from cover. I sighted on the one farthest from the house and put three shots into his chest. The attacker fell down in place and stopped moving. The other three I had spied were looking for the source of my shots but could not locate me since I had ducked down behind the bunker. I took a careful shot at the next attacker in line and scored a head shot that I saw as I dove down behind the tree. I knew that trying to take a third shot from the same spot would be suicide and knew I had to do the scoot part of shoot and scoot. Shots started firing my way impacting the tree and bunker and I knew I had to reposition so I gave Marcus the signal and he unloaded a shot from old Bessy where he saw a muzzle flash shooting at me. I had removed my night vision because I knew what was coming. My wife hit the lights and four halogen floodlights lit up the tree line. The attackers looking our way were instantly blinded and Marcus and I dispatched the remaining three gunmen. We heard a crash at the house and I was up and running instantly. We turned the corner of the house but only saw a body at our front door half draped over the threshold. I told Cindy to go check on Randy with my blow out bag and went back to the rally point. Nobody else was hurt. The dogs were going crazy and bolted for the tree line when they heard cries for help. I heard growling and went to investigate. There was an attacker lying behind a tree with a bloody shoulder.

"Freeze!" I yelled. "Let me see your hands!"

The man was yelling for mercy and kept his hands up. I went over and tossed his rifle away and used a pair of zip ties that I carry on my load vest to bind his hands behind his back. The man was dressed in hunter camo gear, was very dirty and smelled terrible. I was surprised the dogs could not smell him coming but noticed they were downwind of the house and there was a pretty stiff breeze blowing in the night air. He had been hit in the shoulder by Marcus before the lights came on.

"How many of you are there?" I demanded, shoving my rifle inches from his face.

"Six," he said crying in pain.

"What were you trying to do?" I asked.

"We heard you guys had a lot of food up here and we wanted to trade," the attacker replied in a whimpering voice.

"One more lie and you are food for my dogs," I growled. "Where are you guys from and what was your mission?"

"We are from the grange and the tolls are not what they used to be. We heard you were the ringleader of this group and we were coming to take over this area," he said.

"Who did you hear that from and how many are at the grange?" I asked.

"Fifty including us," was his reply. "Just let me go. Some guy named Jones said you were up here and where you lived. We won't bother you again, I promise."

'No you won't," I answered as I shot him in the head. Adam and some of his guards came running to the gate.

"Everything OK?" he asked hurriedly. "We heard the shots and came running."

"Randy has been hit. I haven't checked any of the other bodies yet to make sure they are dead but I know we hit them all. I figured we'd wait around ten minutes to let any fakers bleed out," I replied angrily. It looks like I need a new front door. I looked behind Adam and thought "OH NO, Amy." Adam and I ran up to her house and were pounding on the door. "AMY, it's James!" My heart was in my throat until I saw a flashlight coming down the stairs and I identified Amy.

We checked the other bodies by first putting a 9mm in each of their heads to make sure they were dead. We gathered up the six bodies and laid them out at the foot of the driveway, searched them and took any usable weapons. They were pretty well outfitted and the one that I shot first had good equipment and night vision gear. He must have been the one that led the infiltration and got his fire team past my trip wires. Randy had been hit in the calf with a through and through from what looked like a .22. Fortunately it had missed the bone and any arteries. The bleeding had already stopped but we would send him to our nurse that had relocated to Mr. Jones' house on the Cul-de-sac to make sure there was no foreign material embedded in the wound. Cindy had her arm around Jacob who was standing with his head bowed and tears streaming down his downy cheeks. I went up to Jacob and offered him my hand. "Thank you Jacob." It is a sad day when a twelve-year-old has to take a life, even in self-defense. "I know that it is a terrible thing but it was him or you. He gave you no choice. I hope you never have to do it again but never hesitate."

"No sir," he replied forlornly. "It seems like such a waste. I knew I had to pull the trigger but had no idea how wrong it would feel after."

"I feel the exact same way Jacob," I said giving him a hug. "We do what we have to do to survive."

The family went to bed while I replaced Randy on the roof thinking what a crappy world we now live in and the price young men like Jacob would have to pay with their lost innocence. The rent was just too damn high. The cruel world had just invaded our home and I knew the fighting was just beginning.

CHAPTER 4

The next morning we buried the six bodies away from water over by my septic field, reinforced the front door until a replacement could be scrounged or a permanent fix installed and prepared for our excursion to see Mr. Stutz. We had a hearty breakfast and left Randy and his "bee sting" as we were now referring to it to watch the homestead. I took Marcus, Adam and Jacob with me in an effort to keep Jacob's mind off last evening's attack. I went over the hand signals we would be using on the trail so we could move as silently as possible. We practiced in the woods next to our house with me on point, Adam on second, Jacob third and Marcus at the rear. I pulled out my hunter's ear sound magnifier and we set out with our three day packs and the four bulletproof vests we had accumulated. I knew Mr. Stutz wanted to meet at the Artondale Elementary School based on his rudimentary "Little 'uns AE" code he had given us. I wanted to get eyes on the school prior to our meeting time so we would scout the location and set up good observation posts around the school. We did not have radios so everything would have to be line of sight but any intelligence is better than walking in blind. We dropped off Mr. Black's daily payment on the way and proceeded the two miles to the school, managing to stay in the woods the entire way. I was using a compass and a map of the area that I had used for permitting my property in the past. I also brought a Gig Harbor map out of an old Thomas guide my wife had used from her real estate days prior to the advent of GPS. I managed to bypass many houses using smell from wood smoke and my hunter's ear. We arrived on station at the school at 9AM and set everyone up at hidden observation posts. The school was quiet but there was trash at some of the exits and the doors had been left open. We each had canteens and energy bars and watched our assigned sectors of the school and likely approaches. There were a few dogs at the edge of the playground but we were down wind. Jacob gave me the high sign so I circled back through the woods to his location.

"Sir," he said at a whisper. "There is some movement at the rear door of the school."

I looked through my binoculars at the open rear door of the school and saw a rope tied to the door handle. One of the dogs had been sniffing around the area and when it entered the door, the door slammed shut and a quick yelp was heard inside.

"It looks like we have some dog catchers holed up at the school," I whispered to Jacob. "Keep an eye out and let me know if you see any of our trappers." Just then the door with the rope attached swung open to reset the trap again but I did not see any people.

At noon Mr. Stutz and a group of twelve armed men came down the street on horses and entered the playground. His men fanned out to secure the front porte-cochere of the school. His men were well disciplined and soon had the area secure with good cover and fields of fire. I stood with my arms up, motioned to my squad and walked out of the tree line hoping Mr. Stutz's crew had good trigger discipline.

"How are you Robertson?" asked Mr. Stutz after he had identified me as we walked up and I shook his tree bark hands.

"Not too bad," I replied. "We got hit last night by the group at the toll booth and one of my guys took a .22 to the leg but other than that we are in good shape. Looks like there is a group holed up in the school barbequing dogs. And you?"

"'Bout the same. Jedd, take three men and sweep the school," he replied, turning to one of his men armed with an AR-15. "A bunch in the neighborhood thought they were entitled to my crop and livestock but a few object lessons taught them otherwise. We built a set of stocks at the Arletta store and put any looters or thieves in there for the day. We banish anyone else for more serious crimes like rustling and only had to shoot a couple of rapists. I am keeping everyone fed who wants to work but there isn't much trade except for some entrepreneurial crews out scrounging materials and the old coots fishing off Fox Island."

"We are about the same," I said. "We have lost three. I have heard about a pack of feral dogs, the women's prisoners up at Kopachuck and the toll crew at the Artondale Grange."

"I talked to the women's group," said Mr. Stutz nodding his head. "They are at my backdoor. They were let go when the guards started shooting all the violent criminals in their cells; a nasty bit of work. The non-violent ones were marked and shown the door while the guards locked themselves in the prison using the walls to keep people out rather than in."

"Marked?" I asked, confused.

"They were branded on the backs of their left hands, it looks like a star," said Mr. Stutz. "A little barbaric but they were given a choice, the brand and be set free or a bullet. If they ever came back they would be shot on sight. They are fishing and growing the seed they were sent with up in the State Park and just want to be left alone. There were a few fellows that had the idea of setting up a brothel using the prisoners as the product but the amazons sent them running with a few marks and brands of their own. We need to do something about this toll group. They are right on the road between you, me, the fishermen on Fox Island and downtown. Now don't get me wrong, I am glad those clowns downtown can't get near us, especially after they commandeered my store for the "Greater good" but they are starting to raid and pillage their way into our neighborhoods so we are going to have to flush out this viper nest. They are pretty dug in and have watchtowers and lights on a generator so a frontal assault would be costly. What do you think?"

"Yeah," I replied forcibly. "Six of those fucktards raided my house last night trying to expand their territory. They are pushing up daisies next to my septic drain field."

Jedd came out of the school leading an adult and twelve small children.

"This is Mr. Stewart," said Jedd to the both of us. "He is the science teacher and stayed with twelve of the little ones when their parents didn't come pick them up. They have been living off the food in the cafeteria and vending machines and trapping feral dogs to eat."

"You are a saint Mr. Stewart," said Mr. Stutz, clasping the man's hand and patting his shoulder warmly. "Thank you for taking care of these little ones. How about you lot come stay near my house where we have a small school going."

Mr. Stewart just about fainted in gratitude and quickly had the kids in a line following Jedd and a couple of horse guards towards Arletta.

"I think a quiet flank and rear infiltration would work but we'll need a frontal diversionary attack to distract them before our attack. There is a ridge above their watchtowers by the old water mill that should work for our needs. If you can make enough noise or lob some ordinance their way then we can take out their towers, drop a little fire and send the snakes scurrying," I said, drawing a plan in the dirt with my knife.

"Sounds good. Shall we say three nights from today? Radio call, operation "open road is a go? Over," said Mr. Stutz with a smile.

"They are keeping the City bottled up from us, do you really want to deal with that dumpster fire right now?" I asked.

"Oh, I think we can deal with those carpet baggers if we need to," said Mr. Stutz with a wicked grin.

"Sounds good to me," I said. "Need anything?"

"Some cigars would be nice and a decent bottle of scotch but other than that we are in good shape," he said. "You folks doing OK?"

"We could use some piglets, a few dairy heads and some cracked corn if you have it," I said.

"Done," said Mr. Stutz. "You feed and fatten them then I'll split the take 50/50 with you on the swine. I'll give you two piglets and you only have to return one hog in exchange for two new piglets. You keep the dairy from the cows but I get the meat and any calves. The corn I'll trade for a bottle of 12-year-old scotch and I'll toss in six sheep or three goats for a case of cigars. Fair?"

"Done," I said with a smile. "But the take from the toll rats goes to my side since you are doing the distracting while my folks are doing the fighting. Deal?"

We shook hands. "You drive a hard bargain Robertson," said Mr. Stutz with a smile. "You still owe me $500 from the store."

"No problem Mr. Stutz," I said with a grin. "I always pay my bills. Say, what will you do with the paper?"

"Fuck you," he said with a smile. "Take good care of my girl over there."

"I will," I said. "Take good care of yourself, keep your old ass down and stay out of trouble. I'll see you in three days."

"Bye, over," he said while getting up on his horse with practiced ease and following his mounted men back toward Arletta.

I sent Adam and Jacob back to the homestead while Marcus and I looped around to reconnoiter the grange and the toll taker set up. I knew based on our numbers that we would need a good plan to take on fifty dug in defenders with only fifteen attackers. It would turn into a disaster if we did not have good intelligence and surprise on our side. Marcus and I cautiously approached the military horizon of the hill overlooking the grange. We moved an inch at a time. I managed to find and disable three trip wires and noisemakers during our approach. I knew I would have to completely scour the entire hillside and hope the toll folks did not have a roving patrol. The grange defenses were a three sided bulwark with Wollocet Bay making the fourth side. The grange was in one of the corners of their box and it had to be their barracks. All four corners were equipped with wooden watch tower platforms with a bored looking rifleman perched in each. There were four guards at each of the three gates who were the toll takers for any passing caravans or people. Sixteen total guards without anyone seen outside "the wire." I quickly sketched a layout of the compound and guard composition in my small notebook I always kept handy. I left Marcus to keep watch and slithered down the hill and headed home. I went through the woods to avoid Adam's roadblock and went to my shop to set up a miniature mockup of the compound using my daughter's Lego set and a piece of plywood. I spent the rest of the evening coming up with a plan to overwhelm the nest, running possible scenarios through my mind. I was not a military planner and had no training on how to assault a fortified position so I opted for the simplest plan I could devise to maximize surprise and minimize collateral damage.

The next morning I sent Adam up to relieve Marcus, giving him the infiltration route I had used the previous day and the call sign counter sign Marcus and I had agreed to. I split each of our people into teams of two and explained each of their parts in the mission showing them on the sand table, where they would approach, what they were going to do and when they were going to do it. Each member of the pair had to learn both of their responsibilities in case something bad happened. We did not have radios so the plan either went exactly correct or we would withdraw and have to try a different plan at a later date against a more on guard target. We had snipers, throwers and a back door Trojan horse crew. We drilled constantly for two days and prepared our ordinance for battle. I was optimistic our plan would work but also realistic to know that the best plan only will last for about thirty seconds during combat. The radio sputtered to life around dinner time.

"This is door knocker calling savvybuilder, Over."

"I read you loud and clear door knocker. Over," I replied.

"Condition Alpha," he said. I looked at our code words that we had exchanged at our school meeting. A) Locked and loaded.

"Roger. Time X-ray," I replied. X) Dawn attack.

We left Randy behind to guard the homestead and kids and convened at Adam's roadblock. We knew from Marcus and Adam's intelligence that the guards changed at noon and midnight. We were approaching from the East so I would have the dawn sun at our backs and in the guard's eyes. We sent the scroungers with their old handcarts around the back way through the old mill property so they could approach from the South knowing Mr. Stutz would be coming from the North. The rest of our team cautiously approached the top of the hill. I saw the four scroungers making their way down the street to approach the South barricade gates. The watchtower crew whistled to the gate keepers as the scroungers neared the barricade who opened the gate and stepped forward to inspect the carts and collect their tax. Cindy, Jacob, Adam and I rose quietly from the ridge and fired shots at the four watchtowers taking out the four guards who tumbled to the floors of their watchtowers. The scroungers each took out a concealed suppressed pistol and shot one of the guards who had turned to look up at the noise of the watchtower guards collapsing on the floor and quickly retreated toward the Bay. Just then we heard a huge bang as a head sized rock hit the car barricade from the North. Stutz and his crew had built a trebuchet and had lofted a head sized rock at the wood and abandoned car barricade. His crew adjusted aim and threw the next one right into the barricade gates shattering them from their hinges. An alarm went up from the grange and men with rifles came pouring out of the entrances turning to the north and the source of the loud booms the two rocks had created. Some tried to get to the top of the watchtowers but were cut down by our suppressed snipers and Stutz's fire teams that had infiltrated the woods on either side of the road approaching the north barricade. Stutz's crew kept up a steady stream of fire towards the barricade to keep the defenders' heads down and their focus on the north. I then gave the signal and our "tossers" started throwing mason jars filled with a mixture of gasoline and as much dish soap as we could scrounge in the community. A lit arrow soon arched into the air and set the broken jars' homemade naphtha contents aflame. The wall of fire pinned the defenders between the barricade and the broken gate. The defenders tried to rally and escape through the west side of their box toward the bay but were cut down from the scroungers, the hill above and Stutz's crew to their flank. The fight was over in about ten minutes. The only casualties were two wounded from Stutz's crew who had been hit from a spray and pray from the barricade crew.

Mr. Stutz came riding up brandishing an old six-shooter silver Colt revolver with pearl handles. "All done?" he asked me.

"Looks like it." I smiled seeing him brandishing his six-shooter like the lone ranger atop Silver his trusty steed. "There are six wounded and six who surrendered." I gave the sign and my small tractor came down the street from the direction of my neighborhood.

"You call that a tractor?" asked Mr. Stutz, looking at my garden tractor and whistling loudly. "Now that is a tractor." An ancient rubber tired backhoe came chugging down the street from

Mr. Stutz's group. "Let's get these prisoners of war working on getting this cleaned up. Dig a big hole over by the old water mill and let's get these scum in the ground." He turned to me and asked. "What do you say we take a look in the grange?"

I took Adam, Jacob and Marcus and we stacked up on the door in a line. We went carefully through the grange room by room yelling "Clear" as we finished each room but there were no defenders inside the building. There was a stench emanating from the basement and we quickly found the source. There were six women of various ages chained to the wall in various degrees of undress sitting on soiled mattresses crying. Mr. Stutz came in, took one look, turned to his runner and said, "Add the prisoner work detail to the pile after they are done, no prisoners." We finally calmed the women down and Cindy helped get them cleaned up as best as possible. We found out that one of them was Mr. Jones' daughter so we elected to take her home to our community. The rest decided to go with Mr. Stutz to his. I looked at the loot pile amassed in the main hall and selected a bottle of twelve-year-old scotch and a box of cigars, giving them to Mr. Stutz. "Even?" I said.

"The rest?" he asked looking at the pile.

"Those six women are going to need a lot of help in the coming months. I think a dowry would be appropriate. Let's divide up the ammunition amongst the fighters and let them trade up firearms if they want. Let's take the remaining pile and give each of the women and the two wounded an equal share to help with their needs," I said.

"And the barricade?" Mr. Stutz asked with a nod outside.

"I think we both man it with ten men and ask the fishermen to add another ten. One meal per shift of eight hours. We set up a trading area in the grange parking lot at a cost of five meals per stall per day. If we can find a preacher we can probably have services on Sundays. The grange has a large church bell so if it starts ringing other than Sundays then we will all come running. You barricade Ray Nash Street and I'll barricade Artondale Drive. That will completely isolate us with only three roadblocks," I said. "It is pretty amazing that these old granges are still standing and were originally set up for this very purpose of being a meeting, trading and spiritual center for the community."

"You are a pretty fair minded person there Robertson, especially with the generous dowries. It's a good thing you are on our side. You know those City carpet baggers will be knocking on our doorsteps seeking the equitable distribution of assets and each according to their needs bulldrivel don't you?"

"I'll be sure to send them your way," I replied. "Who is running the fishermen?"

"The Bujacich and Ross crews are running the old coots over there on the island. The downtown Gig Harbor Association tried to impound his boats so he told them to take a flying fuck, grabbed their boats and headed over to Bujacich's place on Fox Island," said Mr. Stutz. "Those old bastards haven't had this much fun in decades. They run the entire Fox Island but are screaming for more diesel and patrol boats for some pirates working up the coast. It's hard to tell if they are serious because those old fuckers are always yelling about something."

"Well geez Mr. Kettle, are you asking about the ebony coating on Mr. Pot?" I asked with a grin.

"Fuck you Robertson," said Mr. Stutz, smiling back. "You had better bring your little Tonka toy over here and pick up your livestock although my cows are both bigger than it is. I also better get a few jars of that shine I figure you're looking to get out of the corn before you feed it to the pigs."

I looked at him a little puzzled, then it dawned on me what Ginny wanted the corn for.

"Aha," said Mr. Stutz. "Looks like age and treachery has once more triumphed over youth and vigor."

Our triumphant crew walked down the street together knowing that our neighborhood and town were much more secure albeit teetering on the edge of starvation. I dropped off the piglets and corn to Ginny at the cul-de-sac and announced that I would cater a party for the entire community down by the roadblock if the food preparers would help set it up. I took our two cows and three goats over to Mr. Black's and helped fence an area of pasture for them and in exchange for rent and pasture space I would give him ten percent of the milk output. Mr. Jones' daughter moved back into her old house along with the nurse who had recently moved in who could keep a professional eye on her. That night we ate spaghetti with ground venison sauce and I even broke out a couple of bottles of scotch to celebrate our victory. The entire town was in a good mood as we planned on consolidating the rest of the town around the nucleus of our community. Anyone could join who wanted so long as they were willing to contribute and trade fairly. I announced our plan for the grange and had the soccer moms post signs regarding an election that was to be held at the end of the month after the harvest was brought in. Harvest time was always a busy time in any farming community as everyone banded together in the fall to get the produce properly preserved for winter use, seeds harvested, cleaned in screens and dried for future use. Our coop chicks were growing quickly and hopefully would begin producing eggs soon and our rabbit hutch was almost ready to harvest the first offspring of our original captures. Our greenhouse was already producing hot weather vegetables like peppers, tomatoes and cucumbers. Our field hands asked what they were supposed to do once the crops were in and I explained how we would have to tend the greenhouse, tan all the hides we had taken, till under the remains of the fields, milk the cows and goats, build a proper hutch for the rabbits…In other words the work on a farm is never done, there is always more to do and accomplish. We would see how our stores fared in the winter months and adjust our following year's planting accordingly.

The grange was a huge success after we had cleared out all the toll takers' garbage. It was used for meetings, classes, worship and as a trading post. We used Cindy's truck with a flatbed attached to drive the five miles of the main road as a taxi service bringing people to and from the grange. We cleared the road of all obstacles and cars so bicycles, horses, walkers and the taxi could all easily use the thoroughfare. We even found a non-denominational preacher for the grange who set up services there and provided a ministry for the community. I had been unanimously elected to be the town mayor with two exceptions, me and my wife's vote. I didn't want anything to do with government. I had selected Adam to be the sheriff and his guards were all deputized. I also selected an old lawyer from up the street to be the judge. There were only five punishments allowed: The stocks; hard labor in our new community garden to be planted at the nine hole Gig Harbor Golf Course; banishment; pay a fine or death. Our town was fertile with some cleared arable land but lots of untouched contiguous wooded areas that were rife with wild game. Our town lands could adequately support its population density but lacked large swaths of pasture land for grazing livestock. Mr. Stutz's Arletta area was flat and full of fertile pasture land. His town had a lot of livestock and farms as a result. What he did not have is enough woodland to keep his people warm during the winter. Mr. Bujacich's Fox Island fishing operation had some farm land, limited pasture but very little fuel since there was only one gas station on the island. The three of us "Mayors" sat down after every Sunday's service at the grange to work out how to keep our towns safe and fed over the winter months. The relative value of resources and medium of exchange for goods and services became the hot topic. Our town had been using bullets as the lowest common denominator for trade. Bujacich was using a pound of fish and Stutz was using silver and gold. We all decided to go to the base metal standard of silver and gold and the three of us would keep track of how much silver was in circulation to keep its relative value steady. A silver pre-1964 quarter became the universal standard for a meal, five bullets or a pound of fish. Currency would make barter and trade easier but a currency only has value if everyone has faith that the currency's value is true. One of our first acts was to set up a local jeweler at the grange who would, for a small fee, meltdown silver and gold and strike coins of a set weight with the stamp AAF signifying Artondale, Arletta and Fox Island. Suddenly grandma's silver flatware and tea set had more value than as a dust collector and semi-annual family polish-a-thon. There is .18 troy ounces of silver in a pre 1965 quarter. We made any struck coins a full .25 troy ounces versus US Mint coins and valued them both the same. A quarter was a quarter again. We struck gold coins at the same weight and used 10X as the value versus silver.

We were sat down at the third post-church service when the pastor came into the meeting room and announced that the Mayor, City Council and Police Chief from the City of Gig Harbor were demanding entrance and wished to speak to us. Mr. Stutz, of course, told the pastor to tell them to "Fuck the Hell off." The Pastor blushed a little red and diplomatically suggested that perhaps the Mayor and Police Chief might be able to provide some insight as to what was happening in the Harbor, on the bridges spanning the narrows and the peninsula gangs rumored to be out by Key Peninsula. Stutz relented and asked the pastor to send the City of Gig Harbor delegation back. The Mayor and Police Chief came into the room. Mr. Stutz and Bujacich were legends in Gig Harbor so they needed no introduction. I was an evil developer so have had some dealings with the Mayor over the years. Many of the politicians backed slowly up to developers and took their campaign contributions while publically railing against them. It was a two-faced system but worked for everyone involved. The Mayor started off with the usual pleasantries.

"Thank you for seeing us gentlemen," started the Mayor. "It seems you folks have done well for us in securing this area. As you may or may not know both the Governor and President have declared martial law and as such the Police Chief, Mr. Andrews here, has been appointed the head of disaster relief and is the acting military governor of this district. I would like to turn the meeting over to him at this time."

Police Chief Andrews stood up. "Thank you Mr. Mayor. Now, here is how this is going to work. Martial Law has been declared and, as acting Governor responsible for this district, my word is final and carries the full extent of the law. First, all food production and stores are hereby nationalized. That means we will be sending crews through the district to collect any food and search all the residences. Food hoarding is now a capital crime. Everyone will be issued a ration card to draw rations at a community run soup kitchen. Second, all firearms need to be surrendered immediately so that our police and militia forces can do their jobs and enforce the laws safely. Third, all fishing is now nationalized so all fishing boats have now become the property of the government. The three edicts go into effect as of this moment. Does everyone understand?"

The room was silent for almost a minute, the oppressive kind of silence like when someone breaks wind in an elevator or a prostitute walks into church. The pin-drop silence was finally broken by a deep belly laugh from Mr. Stutz.

"What are you?" he asked. "Some kind of idjut? Did you just walk in here telling me I had to give you the food off my table, the gun from my hand and row old Bujacich's boats over to you for you to use? Tell me one thing Barney Fife. You and what army?"

"Mr. Stutz, I assure you everything is legal and you are committing a serious crime, punishable by death, for refusing my legal orders," said Andrews who was now red in the face.

"Tell me Mr. Andrews," I asked, "I guess I'm a little slow. I see a few problems with your argument and rationale. That beloved document called the Constitution, that you swore an oath to uphold by the way, says that the privilege of Habeas Corpus shall not be suspended unless in cases of Rebellion or Invasion. You are also looking at eliminating the Second Amendment of the Constitution by infringing on my right to bear arms and if Harry Truman couldn't nationalize the steel industry during the Second World War then I don't think you can seize jack shit. Now, onto other matters, you may have been granted extraordinary powers for the jurisdiction from where you were elected or appointed. We both know that the Gig Harbor City limits are about five miles up the road, you sir, are way out of your jurisdiction. We live in the County and are in no way, shape or form accountable to you. I strongly suggest that you turn back around before Stutz here shoots you between the eyes or Bujacich keel hauls your sorry ass. Now run along, you are dismissed."

The Mayor and Police Chief stood there with their mouths agape like someone had found a turd in the punchbowl. Finally the Mayor gave the Police Chief the nod and the Chief stormed out of the hall. The Mayor turned to us with open arms and said, "Gentlemen, we are starving and need your help."

I growled back at him. "Then get rid of Barney Fife and get someone in here who can give us an accurate status report. Is the Fire Chief out there? He probably has a handle on the situation."

The Mayor nodded, left the room and came back with the Fire Chief. I had dealt with him in the past on building fire suppression systems and knew he was a reasonable though slightly stuffy guy.

"Welcome Chief Winters," I said as the Chief entered the room. "What is happening in the City?"

The Chief sat down and longingly looked at the coffee service on the table. I told him to grab a cup. He poured a coffee, sat back, took a long pull of coffee and began.

"Oh my lord that coffee is good. Thank you. In a nutshell, the City of Gig Harbor is a shit show. The Police Chief managed to stop the food store looting in the five grocery stores and the Costco and we have been using the stores to set up soup kitchens. We issued ration cards to anyone that agreed to have their homes searched for food. The hospital was a disaster area and we lost ninety percent of the patients in the first week. The head doctor was a saint and offered many of the patients that he knew could not be saved a choice, an overloaded syringe and a peaceful death, home hospice if they had local family to care for them or limited care and a lot of pain. Many chose the needle. Pharmacies were all looted since the Police could not secure both the food and the drugs but all the grocery stores have pharmacies so we do have stocks of drugs. There are four geriatric facilities and order broke down there, we ended up with a lot of elderly patients walking the streets with nowhere to put them. Almost all of them died for lack of care. We do have three emergency shelters at the High School, City Hall and have finally got the women's prison guards to let us use the facility as a shelter. They fell for the martial law crap. The Police Chief made anyone entering one of the shelters or receiving a ration card to give up their firearms but that was a disaster as it made the shelters big juicy targets for some of the gangs that now operate in the City. There is a large group holed up at Rosedale gardens and they are using slave labor to grow food in the greenhouses and as a human shield in case of attack. The City has no water except at City Hall and we have been attacked numerous times from gangs from Tacoma. The City of Gig Harbor used to have twenty thousand residents but now there are only two thousand active users of ration cards. We do have communication with the Governor who is located at the State Emergency Shelter in Olympia and the large FEMA camp located at Fort Lewis. City Hall is fully functional since it was built in 2005 and fully compliant with Federal guidelines for hardening against EMP. The City government has been using emergency stores and have housed their extended families in the police station compound. The City does not have running water or natural gas but we bypassed the sewage treatment plant and are back to flushing into the deep water of the bay for sanitation. We have a cholera outbreak brewing and other contagious diseases starting to crop up due to poor diet, sanitation and basic personal hygiene. Some of the older homes with wood stoves are still inhabited but eighty percent of the population lives in one of the three camps. We can only provide one meal and snack per day to the population and we will run out in thirty days. Basically, the City of Gig Harbor is dying. The County, State and Federal Governments have flat out told us that there is no help on the way. The people are on the edge of starvation and ready to revolt. That gentlemen, is the status report."

The Mayor stood up with arms spread, looked us each in the eye and said, "We surrender. What should we do?"

I looked around the room, both Mr. Stutz and Bujacich gave me the nod.

"OK," I began with a deep sigh. "Our towns trade with one another and your current population is about equal to each of ours. We are managing to feed our current people but another twenty-five percent added to the number would kill us all. So we need to figure out how to double our current food production. The City does have some resources that we can trade to help put your population to work. It will be hard work and the Kael eating, Art History Majors and Eco-terrorist crowd need not apply. I think you need to reorganize. Twenty percent will be your food growers. We are too late in the season for outdoor farming but you have access to the two large greenhouse operations, one is under occupation so clearing that out will be a priority. Twenty percent will need to be militia. We need to set up roadblocks and quarantines for both bridges, the Purdy spit and Hwy 16. You also need to rig the bridges and spit to blow in case of emergency. Twenty percent will need to be fishermen and a navy to protect the boats, blockade the two bays and the main harbor entrance to the City. Twenty percent are probably elderly and children, the former will need to educate the latter at one of the schools in the mornings and work at manufacturing products in the afternoons. The final twenty percent will be focused on scrounging, resources and infrastructure. Your main short term resources for trade will be fossil fuels, communication equipment, pharmaceutical drugs, silver, gold and labor. I would strongly suggest working with Mr. Bujacich since there are a few old seiners in the harbor that he can probably crew up but they do call it fishing instead of catching so you need to know where the fish are and not just driving around burning critical fuel. I also noticed there were a few old tugs out there that could pull some barges and act as processing and restocking platforms so the seiners don't have to keep coming back to port, keeping them on station catching fish longer. The only source of food big enough to feed your population is the sea, fortunately the salmon are running right now so everyone needs to pray for a good catch. All four towns will need to make equal donations in food for the militia. The militia will be supplying the defense of all so it is only right that we feed them, it also frees up the manpower currently at our roadblocks to be better utilized producing food. You can redistribute your seized firearms to the militia. The infrastructure crews will need to prioritize getting some of the six local water systems up and running. The large working generator at City Hall will have to be mobilized and stop at each pumping station to fill the water towers. The large water tower centrifuge pumps from the city wells take too much electricity for anything else to run. Turn off every meter supplying unoccupied homes. Large tent city refugee centers won't work. The scroungers need to find every wood stove in the city and get them installed in the biggest unoccupied houses and businesses nearest where they will be working and find every solar panel and inverter they can. If there are any water turbine generators in the City we need to get them installed in the storm sewer main lines so that when it rains we can generate electrical power. The bottom line is everyone has to work for their daily bread and you have a lot of ground to catch up and not a lot of time to get it done. It is not the government's job to tell people what to do, it is the government's job to provide the opportunity to survive. The decision and responsibility to survive lies with each individual. We will trade fairly with you and your people and each of us has pledged to provide one hundred meals daily for the militia. People will starve this winter but if we work hard and pull together we can get through this. We will keep this barricade manned with a skeleton crew to make sure there is no mass migration from the City. You will also have to distribute your emergency government rations to your soup kitchens. We will not support a government that gilds their own lilies while people starve. You guys will have one properly elected official designated to this council, I suggest you hold another election. We will help where we can but each district has to stand on its own two feet. I suggest you distribute some working radios to the three of us and leave one at the grange. Questions?"

The Chief looked at the Mayor and vice versa, neither wanting to be the one to give the bad news to the population. Those that were forced into the camps would be pissed while those that wanted the camps would also be pissed since it was their idea in the first place. Finally they nodded to each other and turned back to the table.

"So what is the going rate for diesel Mr. Bujacich?" asked the Fire Chief.

"A pound of fish per gallon," growled Mr. Bujacich.

"And the price for a pound of meat Mr. Stutz?"

"Five pounds per cord of wood," answered Mr. Stutz. "But bullshit is free."

We went on back and forth for a few hours until the standard weights measures and cost of goods were ironed out between now and winter. We all knew that prices would swing pretty dramatically once the harvest was in and every calorie was accounted for. The City would be the biggest problem since the land was too constrained and the density too large to independently standalone but we would all do our level best to procure enough food to get the population through the winter. We have collectively lost about forty percent of the population with the bulk of the loss in the City proper. These were our neighbors and friends albeit our slightly backwards yoga studio attendee types. The Fire Chief and Mayor left the room.

"What do you think?" Mr. Stutz asked.

"I think we're fucked," I said. "It is all riding on Mr. Bujacich here. The sea is the only place with enough resources until the spring planting season."

Mr. Stutz chimed in. "We don't have the herd sizes yet for the entire population but if we start killing the animals now then we will have a long term problem. My poor bulls and rams haven't screwed this hard in decades. The poor things are going to keel over from exhaustion but if I can double the size of the herd this year and next we will have a chance."

Mr. Bujacich growled. "If that asshole Mayor can get his dick out of Barney Fife's ass for five minutes and get me some gun boats, some diesel and some barges then I can get all ten purse seiners running. Without those fishery ass hats running around I can bring in eight to ten thousand pounds a day depending on the size of the salmon run by netting off the rivers. We'll have to go farther north in the winter so the catch will drop to around five thousand pounds since I will have to tender the catch all the way back unless a crab boat out of Seattle wants to join up with us. The Norwegians are nuts but they are honest and their boats can handle the trip instead of the Mayor's floating sweat shop stink barges."

"Well," I said thoughtfully. "Our total population based on the last census is that we have around eight thousand mouths to feed. I hate to lose any but we will lose around ten percent of the remaining to old age and lost hope. We each have charities of our own in our towns that we are supporting. Perhaps we can help out one in the City if they have some clergy with their heads screwed on straight. I won't donate to the Mayor or the government but if they have a saintly community minded priest who doesn't use the word tithe in every sentence then I'll do what I can and would encourage you both to do the same. Well gentlemen, it has been a pleasure but I have the rest of the crop to bring in, food to process and seeds to harvest."

"You mean my seeds don't you?" asked Mr. Stutz

I took five hundred paper dollars out of my pocket and tossed it on the table. "Here is your five hundred big ones Stutz, don't spend it all in one place. Maybe you can roll those up and light your cigars with them."

"Fuck you Robertson. See, I told you Bujacich, this little tick turd is no good. Say hi to Cindy for me. Damn it Bujacich, quit drinking all my scotch, damn Croatians, always at the bottle, especially if it isn't theirs."

I laughed as I walked over to my bicycle and pedaled home.

CHAPTER 5

The following week we concentrated on pulling in the rest of the harvest. Cutting wheat by hand with scythes was back breaking work, especially when your cutting implement was a modified machete with a shovel handle. The cut stalks were banded, hauled up and left to dry in the driveway where we would thresh them with a modified shovel flail. We quickly learned not to let the chickens free range while this was going on since chasing a hundred chickens away from the grain was like herding cats. We separated the wheat from the chaff and stored the wheat berries in my long term food storage bags. The whole grains would store longer than if we ground it all up into flour. We kept the straw for the chickens, cows, goats and our two horses to bed in. The late vegetables were all harvested and we spent a week straight canning all the vegetables in the pressure canner or water bath depending on the acidity of the vegetables. It was wash, peel, slice and repeat ad nausea but the harvest was plentiful and we were all glad to have it. The kids also harvested all the blackberries on our property and we made preserves and even had a try at making blackberry wine. Randy had devised a Rube Goldberg looking machine that fitted on the rear of the tractor PTO attachment to grind the grain into rough flour and we used the small electric grinder in the kitchen to further screen and grind the rough flour into baking flour. Randy wanted to take the kitchen grinder apart and figure out how to modify his machine but I explained to him that cracked wheat went farther and was more nutritious than baking flour.

"I'm pretty sure the rest of the neighborhood are not making cakes, cookies and pies Randy," I explained. "They are making bread and biscuits."

"OK, sorry," he said with his eyes downcast. "Hey, we promised Ginny we would bring the pressure canner up since none of her posse had any."

"You just want to see Allison the Florence Nightingale nurse up in the cul-de-sac. Don't think I haven't noticed you noticing her."

"Why, did Ginny or Allison say something to you?" he asked excitedly.

"Are you serious?" I asked. "Are we suddenly in high school? Here we are at the end of the world and you are looking for love. Maybe you can send her an emoji text message? I don't think she is looking for a bald plumber who can't pull up his pants or shoot straight. Just sayin'."

"It worked for you didn't it? How Belle ended up with a shit bird like you for a husband is beyond me. Thank God your daughter looks like her mother."

We walked up to the cul-de-sac and saw Ginny holding court with her hen posse. "Now ladies, fill the jars with the vegetables and the juice I made you. Fill these ones up leaving a length of your thumbnail at the top...no, your thumbnail now, not the way they used to be with your French manicure press on nails. Angela, use the measuring stick I gave you and stir out all the air bubbles and fill the liquid to the exact spot I marked on the stick. Good, now Trudy, wipe the top of the jar and pull the lid out of the boiling pan with the magnet I gave you and put it on the jar. Yes, I know you are a bit clumsy so you can put the ring on the top but only screw it down halfway. Now put it in the rack and when you have six ready to go, give me a holler."

Ginny saw us and waved us over. "I have no clue how this species of women ever survived. Did you bring me a pressure canner? Excellent...Randy, please set it up over there. Hopefully these wilting flowers don't blow us up or give us all botulism, it might be a mercy for some of them though."

I laughed. "Ginny, I need some five-pound flour sacks made please if you can get any of these ladies to sew in a straight line."

"How many?"

"Say thirty for now," I replied. "I suppose I could pay you another tub of seeds so you can process the entire harvest this year."

"Done and thank you," she said, giving me peck on the cheek. "I do have a favor to ask though. I don't want to be a bother but I was wondering if you could give me a ride to the services on Sunday. I heard that the hospital is finally under control and I like to ask around about my son."

"Not a problem Ginny. I'll do you one better," I said while pulling my radio off my belt. "This is Savvy builder calling the Chief, over."

"Go for the Chief," I heard over the radio.

"Do you happen to know if there is a Doctor Reynolds working at the hospital? Over."

"Yes, I am just heading that way. Over."

"Can you please tell him that I have a special package for him at church this Sunday? Over."

"I'll pass your message. I hope it is important to be calling me on the emergency line. Over."

"It is critical. Over and out."

Ginny shuffled up to me with tears in her eyes and gave me a big hug. "You have made me the happiest woman alive right now. My boy is alive, my family is safe and I actually matter again."

"Oh Ginny" I said all misty-eyed. "Half of these people would not be alive right now if it wasn't for you."

"Oh stop caterwauling like an old woman," she said composing herself. "Now you and Randy quit messing about, get out of my kitchen and go bring me a deer. Randy dear, Allison is a couple of neighborhoods down tending a cut and won't be back until later so get busy, daylight is burning."

I turned to Ginny with a smirk on my face and whispered, "Does he have a chance?"

Ginny gave me a wink. I saw the trap line crew bringing in the morning catch on some old snow sleds that they had repurposed. The take looked good with Jacob and Marcus looking happy.

"What do you say we go on a hunt the old fashioned way since the crops are in and the deer aren't onto us yet?" I asked.

"As long as Randy doesn't shoot we should be OK sir, he ruins too much meat and I don't feel like chasing a blood trail through the woods," said Jacob with a smirk in Randy's direction.

I laughed. "You know Jacob, there is no such thing as bad students, just bad teachers."

I set up the squad with me on point, Randy middle and Marcus to the rear. Jacob and Allison would hunt to our downwind flank. We ranged well out of our fifteen acres since we had depleted that stock and I wanted it to repopulate. It should not be a problem since we had severely thinned the local predator herd. We headed down toward the grange. I was stalking down a deer trail with my hunter's ear pointed ahead with Randy spaced ten feet behind me when I heard a rustle. I put my fist in the air and everyone crouched down scanning the forest intently for movement. After a few moments I heard "Patriots!" around fifty feet to my front.

To my right flank I heard Jacob say, "Suck!"

"Safe your weapons, we are friendlies," I heard from my front, as six camouflaged armed men with face paint materialized like wraiths out of the forest to greet us.

"DAD!" I heard Jacob cry as he launched himself at the lead person.

Jacob stepped back from his father's warm embrace and said, "Dad. This is Mr. Robertson, he has been taking care of mom and me. Mr. Robertson, this is my dad, Major Harrison."

"Sir," said Major Harrison shaking my hand. "I can't thank you enough for looking out for my family."

"Please call me anything but Sir, Major. I can tell you that the pleasure has been all mine. You have an amazing family. This is Randy, Marcus and Alisha," I said making introductions. "We were just out hunting deer when we happened across each other."

"This is Sergeant Peterson and his ranger team. They are all from the Gig Harbor area. We are lucky you had my son with you since we were at a bit of a standoff there. You must have heard

Gomez over there skinning a deer but fortunately your flank was grouped a little too tight and I saw them and recognized the rifle."

Jacob and Alisha managed to blush the same color red at the same time.

"Please come join us at the homestead for a meal and see the rest of your family," I said. "I imagine the young ones can carry the deer back."

"Please consider it a gift," said Major Harrison. "Is your place covert?"

"Yes and we can infiltrate through the woods."

The expanded squad followed me through the woods. I had never seen such large men move so silently with their heads and eyes constantly scanning for danger. The field hands had already knocked off for the day so it was only the extended family on the patio enjoying a glass of wine in front of the fire while dinner cooked. Cindy came running across our field and leaped into her husband's arms, giving him a full body hug. "I knew you would come!"

Cindy introduced her husband and the squad to our extended family. My wife, Joy and Amy went into the kitchen to expand the dinner meal while Marcus and Randy extended the dining room table for the extra guests.

"We are self-sufficient Mr. Robertson," started Major Harrison with his arm around Cindy. "If you can just point us to a good area to set up camp away from prying eyes it would be appreciated."

"Nonsense," I said dismissively. "Nobody can see in here and I'm sure you and the crew could use a hot shower and a good meal. You can stay with Cindy here in the house and I have a fully loaded 5th wheel about two hundred yards from here where your crew can bunk down. It sleeps six comfortably so they don't have to share bunks."

The Sergeant looked over with a cocked eyebrow to Major Harrison who nodded.

"Well Gunny it seems like God looks out for fools and drunks and since you are doubly qualified it seems to be your lucky day. I promised you a long walk in the woods on half rations and you come out smelling like roses yet again with a hot shower, good chow and a five-star berth."

My wife came out onto the patio and said, "I'm not sure how it works in your Army Major but there are two Generals here and you and my husband are not either of them. Four of you can shower in the house and sooner would be better based on the smell and two of you can shower in the RV. Dinner will be in an hour so you'd best get your muddy boots moving. Laundry goes in the basket outside here, no exceptions. Understand? Can I get a copy that please?"

"Yes ma'am," the Major said with a smile. "You haven't been ruining my wife have you?"

"Major," my wife said with a stern "I will be obeyed voice". "We don't exercise democracy here. This is a benevolent dictatorship and your wife is the other General when I'm not around. If I don't see six sets of fatigues in this basket in the next thirty minutes and six pairs of shined boots you and your men will be turning big rocks into little rocks in my garden. Clear?"

"Yes ma'am," laughed the Major.

My wife looked the other five crew members each in the eye. "Are we clear gentlemen?"

They all came to attention and said in unison, "Yes ma'am, General ma'am."

The squad broke up with the Sergeant and PFC Gomez following me to the RV while the remaining three squad members took their boots off and followed Joy into the house where they were given towels and shown to one of the three showers in the house. I grabbed the Major a scotch and we sat on the patio having a drink while he started wiping his face paint off onto a bandanna.

"She sure is something," he said to me.

"You don't know the half of it," I replied.

"Where is Jacob?" Cindy asked.

"Weeeelllll," I answered evasively. "It seems his dad caught him playing grab ass with Alisha in the woods and made him haul the deer back that the squad killed. I'm not sure if he is figuring out what to say but, in his defense, it was a big buck so he is probably either getting the sleds or quartering it so Alisha can help carry it back."

"That's mean honey," said Cindy with reproach punching the Major in the arm. "She is a nice girl and lives in the cul-de-sac with her mom and grandmother, Ginny. Her dad is a doctor that stayed at the hospital and saw it all the way through to the end."

"Has she been hanging around you and Belle?" he asked with a smile. "Because that would be truly cruel to Jacob."

"Wait until you meet Ginny," I replied with a big smile. "My wife is a minnow compared to that Barracuda. Tell me if you can Major, are you on orders?"

"We are," he replied quietly. "Perhaps if you have some more of this scotch we can sit by the fire and I will tell you a story."

The first soldier came out of the house in a fresh set of fatigues and his used towel, nodded to the Major and started lacing up his boots and repacking his pack.

"Soldier! Freeze right there," my wife said in her command voice from the patio door, waving a spoon at the Corporal. "You get that gear in the basket right now. Now go get your gear squared away at the RV and get those boots clean before you get back. And you," she said, pointing her spoon at the Major. "Get moving. I appreciate the martyrdom of waiting until your crew is squared away before taking care of yourself but I have this handled."

"Copy that ma'am," he said with a smile while his wife ushered him and his gear upstairs to their quarters.

"And I'll only hold dinner for an extra fifteen minutes, your wife wants to talk to you."

A half an hour later the crew came out of the woods all freshened up and the Major and Cindy, both with wet hair, came to join us at the table. Jacob had made it back in time for dinner after dropping Alisha and the deer back at Ginny's. We said grace and dug into a hearty meal of roast beef, mashed potatoes and snap peas. I offered the soldiers a beer but they politely declined until the Major looked at the Sergeant and covertly held up two fingers, then made a telephone gesture. The Sergeant nodded and said, "Gomez and Hannity, you have the watch. Squee, James and Nelson please enjoy a beer."

After dinner the Sergeant turned to my wife and said, "Thank you ma'am, that was the best meal I've had in a long time and your quarters are beyond our wildest expectations. If it is all right, my men and I would like to get some rack time."

"Thank you Gunny," my wife replied. "Breakfast is at 6."

"0600, yes ma'am. We will be here."

"Oh and Sergeant," she said in an off-handed manner. "Can you please count off the contents of that basket over there before you leave? It looks a little light from here in my estimation. I plan to get it soaking before I go to bed so I'd hate to see you try and get past my dogs with a late night incursion after you have mysteriously "found" the missing clothing."

"Yes Ma'am. Sir." He nodded at the Major.

"Thank you Sergeant."

The ladies went into the house and started on the dishes. Major Harrison asked if we could go for a walk to check out the perimeter of the property. I reloaded the scotch glasses and took the dogs for a walk.

"You have a fine place here James. Are you a "prepper?" You don't seem like the sort."

"There is a full range of preppers out there, from the hardcore far right-wing militia survivalists to the suburban tacticool pretenders. I'm more of the Boy Scout variety, with a "be prepared" common sense kind of attitude. I actually took my cues from the Mormon Church prepper doctrine and Alaska off grid mentalities than anything else. I couldn't see my wife sporting camo full time. I knew my homestead was unique so I worked on turning it into my own Alamo."

"You are doing much better than most. Locally, Pierce County is doing OK but Tacoma is a war zone. King County is not doing well, downtown Seattle is on fire, the space needle is on the ground and the eastside is crawling with roving gangs. Snohomish County past Bothell is doing OK. The tri-cities area and Eastern Washington are doing well while Olympia and Thurston County are struggling. We have had little contact with Whatcom County. In a nutshell, any area with a population center greater than fifty thousand people is burning. The Federal government has focused its efforts on getting as many people out of the cities by creating safety corridors to the Midwest and the Mississippi Delta. They figured it would be far better to get the people to the food than vice versa. Without the mechanized equipment we would have had thousands of acres of food and feed rotting in the fields and millions of heads of livestock dying of starvation and thirst. They have managed to get food flowing along rail lines using steam-powered engines but they can't get across the Rockies or the Cascades. The East and West are essentially standalone regions. Texas is Texas. Montana didn't know the power went out and the people of Idaho were glad it did. Utah was particularly well prepared since part of their church doctrine is to store at least a year's worth of supplies and the means to protect it. We are trying to get the desert states into Western California and Texas so the acres of food there can get processed and preserved. We are literally moving the people to the food instead of vice versa. The military has been tasked with guarding the nuclear arsenal and our submarines are on station telling the world that if you attack the continental Unites States, we will turn your country into a slag heap. Washington has numerous bases but the biggest by far is Lewis McChord. It is actually one of the largest bases in the country. Our General there, under the orders of the President has opened the base up to a FEMA camp and kept a small battalion of soldiers to guard the mechanized equipment and armaments. He has sent the Ranger battalions out into the areas that have civilian elected officials to help secure the area and pacify any insurgents. We had heard that Gig Harbor had been mostly pacified and sectored into four towns. My orders were to place four squads covertly, one into each area, to help out where we can. Our General feels that we will be fighting a guerrilla war and that we would be of most use helping the civilian population. I have the overall operational command of the four squads in Gig Harbor and while we can't help logistically, we can help with expertise, communication and co-ordination. I understand you are this towns' elected leader and I would love to hear from your three counterparts."

"So, the army has made you all Green Berets and we are the indigenous population?" I asked.

"Maybe they will give me a Girl Scout hat if I do a good job."

"Well, here is the situation. Old man Stutz, Cindy's boss, has Arletta nailed down. The Crazy Croatian Bujacich is a fish catching machine and will pull all our chestnuts out of the fire come winter. We are doing fine here in Artondale. The City is coming around now that they shit canned the Mayor and voted in the Fire Chief to replace him. We have a gang holed up at one of the greenhouse operations that we need to dislodge, nasty gangs in Tacoma, a women's prison amazon gang in one of our parks that may or may not be friendly, a biker gang on the Peninsula that is pimping out teenagers and some pirates raiding the coast to the North. Add that to my dwindling sex life and we have a tasty shit sandwich on the table."

"Try a massage and some scented candles," he said with a grin. "Can you mark Rosedale Gardens on my map here?"

"Sure," I said pointing to the location on the Major's map. "I have had it under twenty-four-hour observation from here on the map. We have the guard patterns down but anytime the alarm goes up they herd the civilian slave labor they are using to the wire and use them as human shields. I haven't figured out how to breach it without killing half the civilians in there."

"Don't worry, we'll get it cleaned up by the end of the week. I saw the remnants and after action report on your grange attack. Not bad for an amateur."

"How would your crew have done it different?" I asked defensively.

"More snipers and a direct incursion following the Trojan horse back gate takedown. The trick is to never let your enemy know you are even there until they are all dead. You gave them a chance to get organized and counter-attack. We also have flash bang grenades so the grange breach would have been easier. There is no sportsmanship in a takedown, it is all about stealth, speed and instant death. It is sad we are killing our fellow Americans and I never thought my years of training would be used against that goal but you have to put down a rabid dog otherwise the disease spreads to the rest of the pack," sighed Major Harrison.

"Do you need any help taking the objective?" I asked.

"No, but I would like your small group to act as a blocking force and provide a corridor and escape avenue for the civilians in the facility. I'll send my pathfinders in to reconnoiter the objective if you can give them a hand in relieving your scout it would be appreciated since we don't want him to be misidentified as a guard."

"I really appreciate you and your guys being here, it takes a huge load off my shoulders and conscience."

The Major laughed. "As Teddy Roosevelt said, "It is not the critic who counts; not the man who points out how the strong man stumbles, or where the doer of deeds could have done them better. The credit belongs to the man in the arena, whose face is marred by dust and sweat and blood; who strives valiantly; who errs, who comes up short again and again, because there is no effort without error and shortcoming; but who does actually strive to do the deeds; who knows great enthusiasms, the great devotions; who spends himself in a worthy cause; who at the best knows in the end the triumph of high achievement, and who, at the worst, if he fails, at least fails while daring greatly, so that his place shall never be with those cold and timid souls who neither know victory nor defeat."

"Nothing ventured nothing gained?" I asked.

"It's a little more than that. I am a military man who loves his country, that is why I serve. We serve under civilian authority. Would you rather serve under a president like George Washington who has been on the field of battle and heard shots fired in anger or one who took four deferments for the draft due to ankle bone spurs? We used to serve at the pleasure of politicians whose love of themselves was far greater than their love of country. The next generation of leaders will be real citizens, with real problems, not career politicians currently hiding in reinforced bunkers with their families ensuring such worthy goals as the "continuity of government" are met. Do you really think the population emerging from this catastrophe once the dust has settled will endorse their public leaders who hid in a bunker playing their violins while Rome burned? Our service is to the existing American people and the Constitution. One of your first actions was to hold an election and you have fought to protect those that elected you. You could have just barricaded yourself into your homestead but you didn't. Your first thought of the day and last starts with others, how to keep them all safe and fed. There are fifty or sixty squads like mine deployed in the State either making contact with legitimate civilian leaders like you or staying hidden protecting civilians until legitimate leaders emerge. We are all oath keepers who are fortunate to follow a president and military leaders who believe in the American people and know that with the right leadership, resources and mentality, we can rebuild the nation."

"Thank you for the words of kindness," I replied with sorrow. "There is so much to do and so little time to get it done."

"That's why you make the big bucks," the Major laughed. "I am just a trigger puller."

"Oh, I think you are a little more than that there Aristotle," I laughed. "And my first and last thoughts of the day are more of lust than nobility truth be told."

"Massage and candles," the Major laughed.

"I think Patton said that a soldier that won't fuck won't fight," I laughed.

"Well you better get after that there soldier. I'll see you in the morning."

"You too Major. It's great to meet you and I am very glad you are here," I said as we approached the rear patio door. I went quietly into the bedroom where my wife was reading a book by candlelight. "Care for a back rub?" I said to my wife.

"It's like you were reading my mind," my wife Belle said.

Things were looking up as I saw she was already naked under the covers.

CHAPTER 6

The next morning I arose to the welcome sight of a full breakfast table and the smiling faces of my extended family. It was now the second week of September, the canning needed to be finished and the rest of the wheat harvest stored safely away. The weather was getting brisk but the big rains and first frost had not yet arrived. I knew the bulk of the food growing season was behind us so our field hands would have to switch gears into managing and expanding the greenhouse, helping Adam harvest trees for fuel to trade and keeping the predator population down in the woods. I knew old man Bujacich was the key to our region's survival. He was producing over ten thousand pounds of fish a day and had organized the geoduck farmers, small local Dungeness crab boats and even clamming crews for the local beaches. He had told us often that if we could protect the waters and get him some of the crab boats and fishermen from Seattle, he could feed the entire State of Washington. I knew food and safety were the Alpha to Omega of both our problems and solutions for the immediate future. Fossil fuel and electricity production would have to wait. After everyone had been assigned tasks for the day the Major, Sergeant and I went for a walk in the woods to get eyes on Rosedale Gardens.

"Sergeant, you take point, Robertson, you are the salami in the middle and I will take rear. Keep your heads on a swivel and stay frosty," the Major said, looking each of us in the eye. He inspected my gear pulling all the straps on my pack and rifle tight making sure I did not make any noise while moving.

I felt like a rank amateur in the woods tagging along with the two warriors while trying to move silently. These two were like ghosts managing to walk silently while their eyes were scanning the woods in all directions looking for threats. I have some hunting experience but still managed to rustle leaves and step on any branch or twig lying on the ground, creating audible snaps; I cringed every time I accidentally stepped on one. I did see that the Sergeant ahead of me moved with more of a toe to heel motion almost feeling the ground with his toes before putting his full weight down onto his heel so I simply put my feet directly into his footprints and it cut down on the noise considerably. We arrived quietly at the observation point and I gave the existing scout the appropriate sign and he the approved countersign so he would not shoot at us. I looked down from our perch and saw that Rosedale Gardens was humming with activity. There were many civilian people working under the watchful gaze of armed guards planting, weeding, harvesting and watering the various crops inside the glass greenhouses while guards patrolled on foot outside the various buildings. The Major took out a notebook and made a quick diagram of the gardens, took the notes from our observer and left me at the observation post while he and the Sergeant quietly circumnavigated the entire operation. It was 3 PM when the Major returned without the Sergeant and gave me the nod to follow him back to our homestead. I showed the Major the sand table I had set up for the grange operation and he went to work creating a mockup of the gardens. At midnight I attended a scheduled meeting with our "military" at the 5th wheel. The three other five man teams had all made it onto my property and we did not see or hear a single one arrive. The squads were all standing around talking quietly and I gravitated to the Sergeants' group who were standing near the fire.

"Nice barracks Gunny," I heard one of them say to our Sergeant. "Old man Stutz put us up in an old barn at the edge of his property. He came in one night, saw us playing cards, and took five bucks from the squad. We were scrambling around trying to come up with anything silver to pay him with when he told us he'd take an IOU. We figured no problem but the old bastard actually wrote out an IOU form and made us all sign it. I'm a pretty good poker player and have been supplementing my pay for years but old man Stutz cleaned our clocks. We even tried to get him a little tipsy with a jar of hooch we had but the old guy just kept sipping away, smoking his cigar and raking in our chips. Oh look, the Major is here," as he stood up and quietly called the group to attention.

"At ease," the Major said to the twenty warriors all decked out in full battle gear and face paint. There were two soldiers behind him hauling over the sand table. "Simple operation gentlemen and we will go get it done at 0400 this morning. We were going to liaise with the civilian militia in a joint operation but our secrecy and psychological effect will be more important in the long term. Alpha and Bravo squads will be the snipers with two man insertion teams at these five locations. Teams 1-4 are for the eight guards on station located here, here, here and here," the Major said pointing at the sand table map. "Once the roving patrol has been taken down by team 5 then team 5 will take out any pissers. Charlie and Delta teams will breach through here behind the civilian barracks and form a skirmish line to clear any random guards. If no alarm is sounded, and there better not be any alarms sounded gentlemen, then Charlie and Delta will form up at the side entrance to the store, breach silently and clear the main store of vermin. Our intelligence indicates that the store is a single story building with only two back offices and no other doors except the front ones. There are no canine guards and you can assume anything in the main office is hostile. I want this done quick and silent. I don't want the civilians on site to even know we were there. They are on lockdown from dusk until dawn and their latrines are inside their barracks so let's keep them there and they will have a nice surprise waiting for them in the morning. Weapons and comms check in twenty minutes please gentlemen."

The Major dismissed the men, turned and began walking back to my house.

"Psychological effect?" I asked with a raised eyebrow when we were out of earshot.

"If the military takes out a target then everyone feels that the government is here to help them and while that is the case, the help would not be in the form that they want or expect. We need a local legend, something along the lines of Robin Hood, who takes from the oppressors and gives to the oppressed. Only you, Bujacich and Stutz know the military is here, Delta squad, the one I assigned to the Fire Chief, is still covert. The Chief might have been elected but he is not a leader and he is taking all his cues from the three of you guys anyway. Let's get him an asset and see what he does with it."

"Sounds good to me. Where do you need me?" I asked.

"Right next to me," replied the Major. "But don't even think of trying to rub my shoulders."

I turned with a laugh. "What exactly is a "Pisser"?" I asked not being familiar with the term the Major used at the briefing but not wanting to look like a complete noob in front of the professional fighting men.

"More operations have gone sideways because one of the bad guys decides to take a piss at the most inopportune time. Think about it, one hundred bad guys and you expect all of them to have empty bladders at the same time? All you have to do is assign one guy with a rifle to watch the shitter. It's a crappy job but someone has to do it."

The Major and I geared up in the garage and I was handed a fancy radio with an earpiece and a throat mike. The Major showed me how to put on the gear while saying, "Now don't say shit unless there is an emergency. The mike is voice activated. Do not even think of taking a shot unless your life is in danger. You are my rear guard watching my back so I can direct traffic. Head on a swivel and stay frosty."

"Yes sir, Major, sir," I said with a one finger salute.

The squad began the long trek to the first rally point then broke down into fire teams for their insertions to their positions. The Major and I set up in the observation post and he pointed at his eyes and pointed to our rear infiltration route. I looked behind us and mapped out a couple of fall back positions with good cover should we have to retreat or as it is known in the military, "advance in the opposite direction." For the next hour I heard the various teams check in over my earpiece radio, each group designated primary and secondary targets and slowly worked their way into their final positions. At exactly 0400 I heard the Major quietly say "Execute Alpha!" over the radio. The two roving guards at the perimeter simply vanished silently into the woods.

"Execute Bravo!" I could barely hear the sound of ten subsonic rounds over the whisper of the wind through the trees but I did see two guards slump over through my night vision monocular.

"Execute Charlie!" I could see ten of the men coming through the barbed wire that formed the perimeter of the gardens. They moved silently through the gardens encountering no resistance. Two of the men covered the front door while the remaining stacked up in a line by the side door. The point man reached out and slowly opened the door which was fortunately unlocked. The stick of men entered the store and there was neither an alarm sounded nor commotion made. All I heard through the radio were a few gurgles and groans then quiet voices saying "Clear".

We received the all clear thirty seconds later. The sniper crews cleared the surrounding woods and the Major and I entered the wire around Rosedale Gardens.

"Report Gunny," the Major asked.

"Sir, no casualties unless you count the bogies, Gomez twisted an ankle in a pool of blood."

"Thank you Sergeant. Please pile all the bodies outside the front door, find the biggest bad one you can find and string him up by the front gate with this note attached to his body and get the spray cans going. Exfill at 0445."

"Yes sir!" the Sergeant said as he went and started issuing clean up orders.

The next morning the Fire Chief was summoned to Rosedale Gardens and was greeted by a large leather clad, tattooed, bald gentleman swinging from the wooden arches hung by a noose around his neck at the front gates of the gardens. There was a note stuck to the biker attached by a wicked looking knife through his heart. There were a lot of spray painted signs saying "Privateers" around the property. The Chief asked to see the note.

To the people of Gig Harbor:

Beware the privateers! This message is to anyone opposed to a free Gig Harbor. Your days are numbered and we are watching. We are everywhere and nowhere is safe from our vengeance. We are dedicated to a free Gig Harbor!

The Privateers

Great, thought the Chief. Now we have a bunch of wacko vigilantes running around town. The Chief was introduced to Mrs. Kasich, the owner of the gardens prior to the event.

"What happened?" the Chief asked.

"No idea," said Mrs. Kasich. "We woke this morning at the usual start time and nobody came to open the doors. We are not allowed outside on our own. Finally at 10 AM, I opened one of the doors to take a peek and there was no one around. I walked up to the office and all I saw was a pile of bodies and the lead guy hanging from the gates with a rope around his neck. I didn't know what to do so I sent my son into town to get you."

"What do you want to do with all the people you have here?" the Chief asked wearily, secretly hoping they could stay.

"Most of them know the situation outside in the City and were happy to work for their meals. Some want to reunite with their families but most just want to stay and work here, albeit in better accommodations. The bikers have been trading all the food we grow for booze and meat. We are producing a lot of food and have all the seed and resources needed. We could actually expand our operation with some more irrigation and heat. Most of the workers just want to work for a share of the crop and without the bikers it wouldn't take much to double our current production."

"Are any of your people hurt or in need of assistance?" asked the Chief.

"We could use some spiritual help if possible Chief. The women and I have all been raped multiple times and some of the women are pregnant but we are all survivors and I will be damned if those sons of bitches will take away our will to live and survive," Mrs. Katsich said passionately. "We are like a family here who have collectively shared an awful experience but those memories will remain with us and together we can both heal and thrive at the same time."

"Please let us know if we can help in any way Mrs. Katsich," the Chief said solemnly.

"Well Chief, we need people who can scrounge up materials to build more greenhouses, fill them with dirt and work on heating the new buildings. We need people who are willing to work hard to earn their keep. We have given our own blood, sweat and tears into this operation and we will fight to the death to defend what is ours. No other sons of bitches will ever take this from us so long as I am still breathing. I don't know who these Privateers are but I'm glad they are on our side. They have given us the gift of freedom and our lives back."

"I will put together some qualified people and send them your way Mrs. Katsich," the Chief said.

"Send hard workers Chief, not mouths to feed. My family has owned these gardens for three generations and I've been working these greenhouses since I was old enough to walk. There are no free rides," said Mrs. Katsich with authority.

The military squads all returned to their home bases and our team returned to the homestead. There was some confusion when our group returned to the 5th wheel and were searching around for their gear. Someone had cleared out all their packs of dirty clothes and scrubbed the 5th wheel from top to bottom. Every surface and fixture gleamed.

"What the heck Gunny?" one of the soldiers asked, looking into his half empty pack.

"Well Gomez, the rules of engagement were clearly explained to you were they not?" smiled the Gunny.

"I didn't think she was serious," said Gomez.

"Well now she has all your skivvies Gomez so I guess you are going commando until you can negotiate for their release," said the Gunny to his men with a laugh.

"I noticed she didn't touch your stuff Gunny," said Gomez in a whining voice, pointing at the Sergeant's full pack.

"That's because I follow the rules," said the Gunny piously. "Without rules there would be anarchy Gomez."

"What is going on?" asked the Major to the Sergeant.

"Sir," he replied with a grin. "It seems Mrs. Robertson has made good on her promise to perform regular inspections of her barracks that she is temporarily loaning us. It seems some of the troopers are not following her orders regarding cleanliness and laundry sir. Her exact words were "We run a tight ship around here troopers and if I see one speck of dust or piece of dirty laundry in here, I will personally go through all your things and take anything that doesn't meet my standards of cleanliness or decorum." I imagine the troopers thought the military version of clean was the same as Mrs. Robertson's."

"How did you avoid the cleanse Gunny?" the Major asked, laughing openly at the men's dilemma.

"I follow the rules sir. I imagine that Mrs. Robertson kept seeing only my uniforms in the approved laundry basket and came to investigate. It's a good thing she found some dirty clothes or she'd have them all lined up for a VD pecker check thinking they were not changing their clothes. She's a pretty good looking lady Major and there would probably be more than just them standing at attention during the inspection."

"You are a wise man Gunny. Hell hath no fury and all. The troopers got themselves into this mess, they can get themselves out. Let's stand down and get the men out on hunting and foraging parties, we need to earn our keep around here."

"Mrs. Robertson has already provided a ransom note sir. It appears we will be operating a clandestine growing operation out here and that Marijuana is legal in Washington State. She believes that the product will be useful as a pain reliever in the future and wants to be ahead of the curve. She will also trade one pound of clean clothing for thirty pounds of meat."

"Well we don't want to disappoint our host do we Gunny?" asked the Major.

"No sir, she scares me a little bit. I've been dressed down by the best of them over the years and I can tell you that the Bragg Drill Instructors don't hold a candle to her, sir."

"Let's get after it then Gunny and make sure we exceed her expectations in the future."

That evening our extended family enjoyed a dinner together and we discussed our plan for the Sunday services and meetings. The homestead was performing well and the greenhouse was already producing vegetables. The trapping crews were continuing their success and my wife and Cindy were enjoying riding Mr. Black's horses and teaching Amy and Joy to ride as well. My wife was born to ride and is always happiest on the back of a horse. I am scared of the beasts but know that I will probably have to learn to ride in the future. My wife and Cindy were busy altering some of my clothes for the troops, it seems I am the donor because in every case the waists needed to be let in and not out. *Darn ponykeg!* The entire extended family would be going to Sunday services while the troopers would guard the homestead. We were also instructed to pick Ginny and her family up at 7AM sharp. I would make two trips in the tractor with its new extended flatbed.

I arrived promptly at 7AM after a hearty breakfast to pick up a glowing Ginny and her family. They were all dressed up in their Sunday best and Ginny had brought folding chairs, a casserole and three full packs of mason jars for trading. I loaded everything up and enjoyed our slow journey down to the grange. The church service wasn't until 10AM but Ginny wanted a good stall spot for hawking her wares. It turns out she would be selling her white lightning moonshine prior to the services and reunion with her son. It seemed a little odd but Ginny soon saw the creased forehead look on my face and laughed.

"Selling a little sipping whiskey before church have you in a tither James?" she asked with a look of mirth on her wrinkled face.

"I just didn't think it would be a hot seller with the holy-roller crowd," I teased. "I thought the church crowd were more of the tea toting variety."

"I'll have you know that moonshine has always been used for medicinal purposes over the years as a pain killer, disinfectant, analgesic, antifreeze and a cure for the trots. My jars of product all come with a recipe guide for old school uses. You can even run your car on it in a pinch. Judge not there Mr. Robertson, you are next to the house of the lord." She even managed to sound pious in her explanation.

I pre-purchased three jars on the spot for "medicinal purposes only." With the harvest in, the Sunday service was standing room only, albeit with a fully loaded gun rack inside the doors. After the service I headed to the outdoor tea service and was handed a steaming mug ladled from a large pot suspended over a fire. This was my unofficial meeting area where I could talk to various people in the neighborhood and find out if there were any issues or problems that needed my attention. It gave the congregation an opportunity to air their grievances or petition for any changes within the community. I walked over to see Ginny's family, including her doctor son, doing a brisk business at her stall, she was sold out before the post service tea was finished. She had managed to raise prices four times on her product but allowed me in on the original ground floor "promotional sale price." I also noticed Ginny eyeing the other stalls that were bartering everything from bullets to finished fur products. I knew she would have her soccer mom brigade winter sweatshop up and running, turning her tanned hides into finished products and had already cut deals with a fur hat maker and a cobbler to purchase her high quality finished hides and leather. I asked her son and the Major to stick around for the post council meeting which was essentially the real meeting once the Fire Chief left. I took one of the jars of moonshine I purchased and gave it to old man Stutz. He opened the meeting by expertly popping the top of the Mason jar and took a swig.

"Jesus, Mary and Joseph!" He coughed violently. "That's at least 100 proof. You could have warned me you little shit Robertson. Here Bujacich, take a hit off this, you'll be tasting your testicles after this shot in the nuts."

Mr. Bujacich took a swig stoically but even his Croatian constitution had to gulp for air.

"Major?" he asked passing the bottle.

"I'll take a hit, my parents are from North Carolina you know and sipping whiskey is part of our heritage." The Major took a small sip as if sampling a fine wine. "Pretty smooth for a Yankee," he declared, offering Ginny's son the jar.

"Ah no thanks," the doctor replied with a smile. "My mom always said I was going blind from a different youth pastime but I'm pretty sure my poor eyesight was caused by her sipping whiskey."

I took the proffered jar from the Major and took a swig. "Smoooothe," I croaked with my eyes watering. "Well doctor, we have heard the Chief's version of the City and figured we needed a less rose colored glasses version."

"First, I can't thank you all enough for taking care of my family during these trying times," he began solemnly. "My mother hasn't been this energetic and engaged in years. The City is a dumpster fire. When the shit hit the fan, everyone wanted the government to do something and being good little politicians they elected to nationalize everything. Last month they did an about face and tried to privatize the collective which essentially made everyone mad. It's a good thing they took everyone's guns away before they told everyone there would not be any more government run refugee camps and everyone had to work for their food. Thank goodness the tent camps were shut down because we had both a Cholera and E. Coli breakout at all the camps. There were just too many people living in poor conditions, with a poor diet and no sanitation to work. Almost all of Gig Harbor North is empty. There are over a thousand new tract houses up there but they are all on postage stamp sized lots and the entire master planned community is on sewer lift stations so all the sewage backed up into their homes when the electric pumps stopped working. The Canterwood golf and country club gated housing community fared much better and most of the golf course is now pastureland or is in food production. Downtown is doing OK with a lot of the old Croatian families banding together and getting organized. They were always fairly independent, ignored the government and took to the water in small fishing vessels. Rosedale Gardens was liberated by some vigilante group called the Privateers but nobody can figure out who did it. The gardens were a treasure trove of talent though and the City is actively working on expanding their operation. The hospital is still taking care of a few patients recovering from things like broken legs but all the doctors have decided to set up practices in each of the communities and form our own association, helping each other out when needed. I will be working with Allison, a nurse from my neighborhood here at the grange. I am a board certified cardiothoracic surgeon but now I am a General Practitioner using skills I haven't practiced since my residency. There isn't a big call for heart surgeons these days. The Narrows Bridges see daily sniper activity from Tacoma since the gangs have blockaded their side of the bridge too but the Peninsula biker gangs seem content to stay put."

"Thank you Doctor Reynolds," I said thankfully. "I appreciate you giving us your perspective and I'd like to be the first to say welcome to our neighborhood and kudos to you and the medical community for working together and finding your own solutions. If you'll excuse us, we have some other council business to attend to."

The doctor left the hall and went back to his loving family. I paced the room in thought. "You know this all comes down to you Mr. Bujacich, don't you?"

"Diesel," was Mr. Bujacich's single word reply. "The Chief has around ten thousand gallons left which puts us on station fishing for only another two months. If the pirates out of Seattle's Elliot Bay and the Port of Everett would leave us alone then we could stretch what we have another thirty days since we wouldn't have to go through deeper waters to get around them. The Chief's protection boats don't have the fuel capacity or free board to get to deeper waters so they are just monitoring the pirate bays. If they give us the warning signal then we have to pull up our nets and get to deeper water which also costs us fuel and fishing time. The sad part is that if you could get me the Norwegian crab boats out of Seattle and enough diesel, we could feed most of the State of Washington and parts of Oregon too. We also need refrigeration. We can only smoke so much meat before we run out of salt."

"Any ideas Major?" I asked, turning to the military man who was sitting pensively at the table.

"Do you know where the pirates are moored and operating out of Captain?" the Major asked Mr. Bujacich.

"There are only two marinas where they could be stationed," Mr. Bujacich replied thoughtfully. "The Elliot Bay Marina by the Magnolia Bridge in Seattle and the Port of Everett Marina. We have seen six older yachts around sixty foot with three pirate boats operating out of each marina. There are not that many deep moorages with the dock length to moor that sized boats."

"Can you show me on a map where they would be?" asked the Major, producing a map of the Puget Sound.

"Sure, come on by my boat and I'll show you on my charts, they will give you a clearer picture," he replied.

"If hypothetically a barge with 100,000 gallons of diesel were to show up, where would you put the barge?" asked the Major, looking back at his map.

"I'd anchor it right in the middle of Gig Harbor Bay," said Mr. Bujacich. "The Chief has the mouth of the bay blockaded but if one of "his" boats, which are actually my boats, were to mysteriously find such a barge then the blockade guards would let it through."

"Where would I find all these Norwegian Vikings?" asked the Major.

"They all live in Magnolia on an island outside of Seattle. If I was a betting man they will have blockaded the bridge. They are as tight as ticks over there. If you've ever seen the show "Deadliest Catch" then you will know who all the ring leaders are. Over half of their boats are tied up in Alaska while the other half that need more maintenance and overhauls are tied up at Fisherman's Wharf near the Ballard locks in Seattle. The big crab boats can hold up to two hundred thousand pounds of catch in their holds and they used to spend the early fall season tendering our catches to the processing facilities in Alaska before crab season started. We used to have to steam up near Alaska for our catch due to regulations but it is easier to work the river basins where the fish are actually going to spawn instead of trying to intercept them between points A and B."

"So diesel, protection, refrigeration and Vikings are our short term problems," recapped Mr. Stutz. "What are our long term issues and solutions?"

"Well," I said. "Washington State accounts for 25% of the nation's hydroelectric power generation and all the dams predated solid state electronics. The biggest dam is the Grand Coulee on the Columbia that was built by Roosevelt during the Great Depression. 75% of our state's electricity comes from hydroelectric power. I'm sure the dams can still produce electricity but all the transformers that stepped the power down and converted it to usable AC power will be shot as well as the grid that distributes it. Washington is also the fifth largest petroleum refining state refining all the oil coming out of the Alaska pipeline. With electricity and petroleum we can restart manufacturing, processing, refrigerating and shipping goods across the Pacific Northwest, assuming all the gangs, thugs, warlords and despots out there let us."

"Well thank you Cliff Clavin for your obscure knowledge of Washington State trivia," said Mr. Stutz with a chortle. "So that is our medium term goal. Once the Chief mysteriously finds

100,000 gallons of diesel to trade to the Captain for sushi and the Major finds the Vikings then we can magically rid Tacoma and the Key Peninsula of fucktards and we can turn on all the lights. Sounds like a pipedream on top of a circle jerk to me. Looks like Ginny's shine has knocked a few screws loose."

"A man has to dream Stutz," I replied with a smile. "This morning my only goal was figuring out how to get laid and now it's how to save the world. One out of two isn't bad."

"Well you better get your hand off your tiny pecker and get around to seeing the Amazons over at the park. The Major's Privateers might have to sign on for another mission," said Mr. Bujacich.

"I think we all need to go," said the Major to the group. "We might be able to stave off any conflict with them if a diplomatic solution can be arranged, although I don't think diplomacy is any of your strong suits."

"Fuck you Major, how you ended up with Cindy is beyond me," said Mr. Stutz with a grin. "Then let's shake a leg, I've got better shit to do than stare at a bunch of women ex-convicts."

The four of us loaded into Mr. Stutz's truck and stopped off at my homestead so the Major could brief his squad and set them up in over watch positions at the entrance to the park for our meeting. My wife provided lunch and I gave Mr. Bujacich and Stutz a tour of my facility. My wife played the usual game of Gig Harbor relations with our guests.

"I knew your grandfather and grandmother, Belle. They ran Marcus's Tavern down by Jursich Park didn't they?" said Mr. Bujacich. "All the captains used to hang out there in the offseason."

"Yes," said Belle. "The tavern was named after my dad Marcus here."

"Is that you Bujacich?" Marcus asked walking up to the group shaking hands.

"Marcus!" Mr. Bujacich said giving Marcus a big bear hug. "Still have the old place on Harborview? Your mom was one of the greats. Her parties during the blessing of the fleet and annual parades were legendary. I have never been so drunk in my life dancing around with the accordions playing their darn Croatian songs. Remember that summer you and your brother worked on my boat and you fell out of the tender?"

"Sure do!" Marcus replied with a big smile. "That was one hell of a summer. We still own the old place on Harborview but lord knows what kind of shape it's in now. What are you old boys up to?"

"Going to see the Amazons over at Kopachuck," said Mr. Bujacich

My wife overheard the reply and said, "You four must be the dumbest men on the planet. I've seen my husband look longingly in the prison yard, while driving by, thinking how sexually repressed the prison population must be and how he must be the answer to their nightly prayers. Your little sausage factory visit stands about as much chance of success as a snowball in hell. You'll probably end up starting a war with those ladies and I'd probably be on their side. What makes you possibly think they want or need your help? The whole knight in shining armor meets damsel in distress won't work. I'm coming with you and will be doing all the talking, you all stand there and look as stupid as you seem to be."

"Honey. It might not be safe," I tried to reason with my defiant wife. "We don't know what we are walking into."

"I have to," my wife said with her jaw set and little foot hopping. "You four testosterone bulls will be thinking with the wrong heads. I want peace not war. I'm sure the Major's men will keep us safe. Besides, we'll just tie Gomez's dirty skivvies to the truck antenna to be our white flag as the universal symbol of peace and male subservience."

"Ok," I said ruefully. "But at the first sign of trouble you are to fall back to the truck and do exactly what I say."

My wife agreed to my rules of engagement but I'm sure her fingers were secretly crossed behind her back. We received a status report from Gunny that his crew was on station, loaded up the pick up and started for the park. My wife held a cardboard box on her lap that she had packed for our meeting.

"Pretty nice set up there Robertson," said Mr. Stutz as we were leaving the homestead. "Looks like my chickens are about to start laying. I like the wood gas set up. Can you make me a couple of those gasifiers?"

"Randy is the engineer, I'll send him over," I replied. "I'm sure he can hook you up for a reasonable fee."

"Fuck you Robertson," said Mr. Stutz. "I hope they are homing chickens and all fly back to my store."

"I did pay you your five hundred dollars if you recall," I said with a smirk. "There is no such thing as a free lunch."

My wife held out her hand to Mr. Stutz who was seated beside her. "Twenty-five cents please."

Old man Stutz dug around in his pocket for a quarter but all he could come up with was a gold coin while swearing under his breath.

"Honey," my wife said to me. "Mr. Stutz needs some change or I suppose he can just owe it to me."

"You're a cruel woman Belle and a chip off your old grandma's block. There's two things I know about the Klenak clan: don't bet at cards with them or you'll lose your shirt and don't mess with their women or they'll hand you your lunch. I used to be sweet on your grandmother in the old days but she always said I should never enter a battle of wits unarmed."

We arrived at the Kopachuck State Park entrance with a white flag flying high out of the window. The entrance to the park was barricaded off with a substantial wall of trees and abandoned cars. I was a little nervous because we had passed some signs on the way in saying "Warning, no entry, white flags will be fired on." A guard came forward with her hand up in the universal sign of stop. There were at least ten guards behind the barricade with rifles all trained on us. We stopped and all put our hands out the window.

The stopping guard came forward and told us all to get slowly out of the truck. "Thanks for the new truck, you illiterate dumb shits. Leave your weapons in the truck, turn around and walk back the way you fucking came."

I stepped forward with my hands still in the air. "We are the leaders from Gig Harbor and just want to talk. We mean you no harm."

"Yeah," the tall woman with long black hair of Native American descent said. "Just like every other prick that comes by. We just want to be left alone. There, we have talked, now fuck off."

My wife stepped around me and slowly walked up to the guard. She stepped right up to the guard, put her arms around the lady and gave her a hug. The guard stood stiffly for a few seconds but then returned the hug.

My wife turned to us. "Now, you four just stand there like good little boys while we go have a chat. Honey, move very slowly and get my box out of the truck. That's a good boy." My wife turned to the guard and whispered something to her and the guard answered back. "Deirdre and I will be a little while so why don't you boys go sit on that log over there on the other side of the street and try to not look stupid or embarrass me. Ladies," she said to the guards. "If any of them twitch you have my permission to shoot their peckers off. I hope you have scopes because they might be hard to find in their current frightened cold water state."

My wife followed Deirdre to the entrance guard shack and they both entered. The four of us just sat like four bumps on a log across from the entrance.

The Major whispered, "This will be a tough extraction if it turns ugly."

I replied, "Trust her. All women seem to share a collective brain. They'll be organizing a bunco party and exchanging recipes in no time. I'm sure her little care package includes all the requisite klatch building tools like wine, cheese and baby pictures."

After an hour my wife and Deirdre exited the shack. My wife turned and gave her another big hug which was warmly returned. She pointed at the four of us, whistled and pointed at the truck. We hurried over at her beck and call and quickly piled into the truck.

"Did you join their tribe?" I asked.

"I was already in their tribe," my wife replied. "They wear their brands as a badge of honor joining them in sisterhood. They just want to be left alone. Their rules are simple: No men and no men. They would like the ability to trade with our towns, they would like to see if there is a female reverend to start a ministry and they want to be treated as equals. I'm sure a proclamation of some type at the grange would do wonders and I offered our taxi services to bring any that are so inclined to the grange. These are proud women who won't put up with any disrespect and it's up to you four to make sure there isn't any. It seems the prison system actually provided them some valuable education on independent living. They are already survivors and have natural hierarchies already in place from their time in prison. Bottom line is they are no different from any strong independent women out there who had enough common sense to swear off men."

"Good job sweetheart," I said with affection. "It looks like peace without a shot fired in anger."

"Yes dear," she replied. "If women ruled the earth we wouldn't be in this mess. Now take me home, I have some dinner to get started. You will be joining us, won't you?"

"Will it cost me another quarter?" asked Mr. Stutz with a chuckle.

"No. I'll just add it to your tab. Maybe we can have a couple of hands of cards after dinner. I heard you took some of the soldier's lunch money over there Stutz."

"Um no," said Mr. Stutz. "I once almost lost my finest bull to your grandmother."

"Shit!" said Mr. Bujacich. "You must be pretty good at cards Stutz, I almost lost my boat to her."

"Oh and gentlemen," said my wife to the whole crew. "You need to bring your significant others, either wives, daughters or sisters to church next Sunday. You know who I mean; the ones really in charge of your little operations. It is time the ladies all got organized and got this shit running smooth so you jagwhistles don't fuck it all up again. You would have got your balls shot off today running around half-cocked like you were planning to."

We all went back to the homestead and enjoyed a great meal of steak, fried potatoes and corn. The jars of moonshine were liberally handed around. After a dessert of apple cobbler my wife pulled out a deck of cards and asked, "Tell me again, does two pairs beat three of a kind?" The Captain and Mr. Stutz roared with laughter and beat a hasty retreat. We had one of the Major's men drive them home in Mr. Stutz's truck since even their incredible constitutions were overwhelmed by Ginny's white lightning.

My wife and I were getting ready for bed when I gave her a big hug.

She said with a sigh, "Can we really turn this thing around honey?"

"You did a great thing today honey. Edmund Burke once said "The only thing necessary for the triumph of evil is for good men to do nothing." All we can do to eat the elephant, is take one little bite at a time. There is so much pain and suffering in the country right now and all we can do is control what is in our control and hopefully expand from there."

CHAPTER 7

ALARM! I abruptly shot out of bed to the sound of my dogs barking at 2 AM. I shook off the cobwebs and shouted for my wife to get up. I heard gunfire erupting all around the house. I quickly tossed on my gear, grabbed my rifle and ran to the rally point. As soon as I opened the door, bullets began impacting all around me as I dove behind the rally point fortification we had erected. The gunfire was coming at a steady pace from the driveway thumping into the barricade in front of me. I also heard gunfire from the front of the house coming from Mr. Black's property. The Major, Jacob, my wife and Cindy were trapped at the doorframe I had just dove out from. I looked to my wife and motioned for the lights on three. She nodded and flicked on the floodlights to illuminate the driveway. The Major followed me as I ran to the driveway fortification while my wife, Jacob and Cindy got behind the rally point barrier and began firing at any exposed attackers. I took a round to my right arm as I dove behind the driveway barricade. It felt like I had been kicked by a mule.

"Jacob! Sniper! My eight o'clock in the cedar tree on three," the Major yelled back toward the rally point. The Major and Jacob both shot suppressed rounds at the same time and a black-clad sniper tumbled out of the tree. I checked my arm and was relieved to not see arterial blood gushing.

"Robertson, covering fire!" the Major yelled to me. "Lights out in three, Jacob, start on the left side and I'll roll them up from the right."

I came to one knee and began firing at muzzle flashes until the floodlights went out. I pulled down my monocular and saw the Major working up the attacker's skirmish line, delivering three shot automatic bursts at the attackers who were trying to get their own blinded night vision gear back online. Jacob and the Major yelled clear and we quickly ran back to the rally point to help our military squad who were pinned down. The Major had us stack up on him at the front corner of the house and took us right into the attackers' flank in a skirmish line. The battle was over quickly once we were able to unpin Gunny's squad and his team advanced through the attackers while they were trying to adjust to the Major's vector of attack.

"Report Gunny!" the Major said over the radio.

"I have one down and one unaccounted for Major, sir."

I ran to the rear patio and saw Randy down, he was not breathing. I quickly peeled the vest from his chest and began giving CPR. I glanced up and down his body and did not see any blood seeping from obvious wounds. Finally after two rounds of chest compressions he coughed and began breathing on his own. We found Marcus in the front yard down writhing in pain from a fractured leg he received when he had fallen from the sniper perch on the roof after taking a single shot to his bulletproof vest. My wife and Cindy with Jacob guarding them went to get the doctor and Allison the nurse while Gunny's men made sure the downed attackers were all dead.

I sat down heavily on the concrete patio and pulled out my blow out bag to staunch the bleeding from my arm while Gunny's crew improvised a stretcher using one of the patio chaise lounges for Marcus and Randy, who was starting to come to. The Major was on the radio putting the other three teams on high alert.

I turned to the Major and asked, "Whiskey Tango Foxtrot." The universal military question of What The Fuck.

"Looks like two ten man, well trained, fire teams. They took out the Black's house, Amy's house, Gomez who was on perimeter patrol and our two house guards. This was a well-coordinated attack and if it weren't for your dogs and lights we'd probably all be dead. The attackers were all armed with incendiary devices and their plan was to take out the guards and burn down your house with everyone in it. These were professionals based on their tactics and their gear. I'd say SWAT. We have been hearing rumors that one of the Tacoma crews had a SWAT team as their muscle but I wouldn't have believed it until I saw it."

"The Blacks and Amy?" I asked with a trembling voice.

The Major shook his head. "They used knives sir. It isn't pretty. I am sorry I failed you, sir. I underestimated our adversary and almost paid the price with both our families' lives."

The Major turned with tears in his eyes but perked up when a new voice came into his headset. All I heard was "Yes sir. No sir. No sir and 0600, yes sir, over and out."

"It looks like we lost the Fire Chief, sir. This crew came here directly from downtown. They are based out of Tacoma and were planning on taking out all four community leaders. They have maps and layouts for Mr. Stutz, Bujacich, the Chief and you sir. They were planning on decapitating the entire command and control of your community. They were coordinating with the Olympia capital gangs and it appears the Governor's bunker was breached and all hands were lost. The General would like to see you, the Captain and Mr. Stutz and will be sending a boat to Mr. Bujacich's compound at 0600 this morning sir. The Bravo team from downtown is coming here to protect your family and home."

"Will you bet your family's lives on Bravo team Major?" I asked, looking him straight in the eye.

"Yes sir I am and will," said the Major with confidence.

Doctor Reynolds came up to me to inspect my arm after he had checked out the wounded soldier, Randy and set Marcus's leg fracture. I looked at him with a raised eyebrow. He replied, "The soldier took a shot to the wrist and will need some extensive surgery to repair it. He is stable. Randy had a blunt force trauma to the chest that stopped his heart. He has one hell of a bruise and three cracked ribs but no internal bleeding. He's damn lucky he had a vest on, you know CPR and the firefight was over quickly. Marcus has a compound open fracture to his tibia and fibula but there is good circulation to his toes. He will need a cast. Your arm is going to hurt like all hell for the next six weeks since it went right through your bicep muscles but it missed the bone and just missed your brachial artery. I'll sew it up and if you promise to keep it immobile, I'll put it in a sling instead of a cast."

"Thanks Doc," I said. "Just use a local if you have it. I need to take a walk in the woods and need my head clear in case there are any more of these bandits out there."

My wife came over to inspect the doctor's work. "Amy and the kids, the Blacks, the Chief and Gomez?" she asked with tears in her eyes.

"Yes honey. I'm so sorry," I said while giving her a big hug with tears streaming down my own cheeks. "I need to take a trip with the Major here. I should be home for dinner."

"The hell you are. You've been shot for god's sake and there are thirty bodies lying around our yard and my house is all shot up."

"I need to do this sweetheart. Bravo team is coming over to keep the house safe and I'm sure they will help put it all back together until I return. You've always been busting my chops to remodel so get after it. Please see to Amy and the Black's arrangements. The shitheads that did this know where we live so we can wait here for them to come again or we can take the fight to them."

"You two better go find those shit birds and carve out their hearts with a rusty spoon and don't bother coming back until you do. You keep him safe Major. I don't want you two out there doing something stupid, playing cowboy. Copy that?"

"Yes, ma'am," was both our replies. My wife gave me a hug and a kiss. She went over to the Major and gave him a peck on the cheek and pointed her finger at his nose. "Copy that," was all he said with a nod in her direction.

The Major went through my gear and asked where my spare night vision goggle batteries were.

"I just replaced the one in there Major," I replied with a whine.

"Two is one and one is none," he replied.

"I thought ounces equaled pounds and pounds equaled pain?" I said sagely.

"What would you rather have? The ability to see in the dark or your teddy bear to snuggle at night?" he asked, pulling one of

Avery's's stuffed toys out of my bag that she constantly put in my pack to keep me company.

"I'll get some more batteries," I replied with a chuckle.

"Gunny!" the Major said. "Form on me."

The Sergeant came up to us and stood at attention. "Sir!"

"Gunny, you are in charge while I am away. Everything that is special to me is under your care."

"I will guard them with my life sir. I would like to apologize for..."

"Stop right there Gunny. We were attacked by twenty highly trained men with surprise on their side and we only lost one man and have three non-critically wounded. They had advance knowledge of our strength and defense, were well armed and executed a textbook take down. It was only our quick reaction and skill that avoided a massacre here today. You and your men performed extremely well resulting in their side dying for their cause rather than us for ours. I want this carnage cleaned up and checked for intelligence before the sun comes up and before the field hands show up for work and get those two dogs the biggest juiciest bones you can find. We owe all our lives to Caymus the ridgeback and that wheezing slobbery Hunter."

The doctor gave me a bottle of Ibuprofen for after the local wore off and the Major and I began walking toward Fox Island. Fortunately the Major had radioed ahead and his Fox Island squad materialized once we were past the Fox Island bridge barricade with bicycles for the Major and me. My arm was just starting to throb in earnest when we pulled up to Mr. Bujacich's compound. Mr. Stutz was already there with a stogie stuck between his teeth.

"Those fuckers want to come to our house?" growled Mr. Stutz, chomping on the end of his cigar. "Send the next ones my way and I'll give them something to cry about. I feed the fuckers alive to my hogs just to hear them scream!"

"We'll deal with those ass hats," I said with conviction. "I have a special rusty spoon my wife gave me."

"Hey, it's 0600," said Mr. Bujacich. "Does your Navy not have a working timepiece?"

Just then a small Coast Guard patrol boat came gliding up to the pier.

"Don't you scratch my pilings you safety Nazis," yelled Mr. Bujacich to the oncoming vessel.

"Ahoy Captain Bujacich," was heard from the bridge.

"Smitty, is that you, you asshole?" cried Mr. Bujacich, peering into the wheelhouse. "Now we are truly fucked. This landlubber once wrote me a ticket for having expired fire extinguishers on my boat. Hey Smitty, let me see your fire extinguishers." As he expertly hopped on the deck before a single line had been attached and made a beeline for the wheelhouse. The rest of us piled onto the deck. The Major started the whole salute and permission to come aboard when Bujacich's voice came from the bridge. "Stop that nonsense Major. I knew Smitty when he was a twerp tender operator on my boat. I am the senior seaman aboard this vessel and have had my papers since before Smitty was the load his mother should have swallowed was shot. Get this tub of shit moving Smitty. Hey, does you boson have one of those little whistles. Get him to blow that."

Bujacich was in his element as we made our way over to Steilacoom Harbor. Tacoma was aglow with various fires burning and smoke in the predawn light. We were met at the pier with a full platoon of riflemen and ushered into two electric dune buggies for a silent ride to the army base and were whisked through two heavily fortified checkpoints on our way to the army base command center. We were ushered into the building and were greeted by a general dressed in fatigues. The general was a tall distinguished looking man in his mid-sixties but did not possess the pony keg that I had strapped around the middle. The general wore two gold stars on the cap he was wearing, his breast name plate read Holcomb, and came up to us giving each of us a warm firm handshake. "As you were Major," the general said as he ushered us into a large conference room surrounded by monitors with various maps of the state, country and world around it. There was a large weathered face on the live feed of one of the wall monitors and another military man on a different screen.

"Welcome gentlemen," General Holcomb began the meeting. "With us is Mayor Jackson of Spokane, General Young from Fairchild Air Force base and with me here are Mr. Robertson, Bujacich and Stutz of the Gig Harbor area."

"Is that you Jerry?" asked Mr. Stutz of Mayor Jackson.

"Sure is Stutz. How they hanging? Remember those dancing girls at the Vegas farmer's convention?" the man on the video screen answered.

Mr. Stutz laughed.

"If I may gentlemen," the General began. "As you know the Governor is dead. You four gentlemen represent the only legitimate elected officials we can find in the entire State of Washington. I brought you all together to give you a briefing on the status of the State and the country. As you know we have multiple squads of soldiers deployed in many different parts of the state. They are called angel teams. The President felt that our military would be best deployed as guerilla forces rather than a homogenous unit assisting local groups against roving bands and helping the local populations. All of our strategic nuclear forces have been secured to act as a deterrent against any foreign incursion. Our borders are secure except for a large band currently invading from our southern border with Mexico. The drug cartels have all organized and are trying to infiltrate into border towns. The omnipotent wall seems to be a poor deterrent. We have motorized brigades deployed and have secured the border. We have broken the country into four zones with the Ohio and Columbia rivers demarking the North South Line and the Rocky Mountains the East-West line. In a nutshell the Southeast and Northwest are holding their own. The Northeast and Southwest are struggling. We estimate the entire population of the United States has gone from around 350 million to 150 million. Washington State had around 7.1 million people before the event, we estimate that number is closer to 4 million now. The Governor's mission was to open a corridor from Eastern to Western Washington and get as much food that could be harvested shipped west. We were running the tonnages we could ship but without a rail line we can't move enough food west to feed the population."

"Well," I said interrupting the General's presentations. "It looks like the Governor's single death might have just saved a few million lives."

"Mr. Robertson?" asked the general. "Would you care to elaborate?"

"I would imagine that without combines Mr. Jackson over there will lose over three quarters of his wheat harvest and without grain the Montana and Wyoming ranchers will lose half their herds. Gentlemen, it is now the first week of October and Mr. Jackson probably has about two weeks before his crops start rotting in the fields. You are wasting assets trying to move the mountain to Mohammed. We need to produce the biggest migration in these parts since the gold rush. Two questions General. How many people are in these FEMA camps and how many unharvested acres does Mr. Jackson have?"

"There are currently almost 100,000 people in this refugee camp Mr. Robertson," replied General Holcomb.

"We have over 100,000 unharvested acres," supplied Mr. Jackson.

"General," I said. "We need to move 100,000 people 200 miles in the next 48 hours."

"Mr. Robertson, with all due respect, the three mountain passes are impassable due to dead vehicles and fortified blockades. The President of the United States tried a similar maneuver in the Midwest and while some lives were saved, there was no infrastructure to house the migrants, feed the migrants or process the food harvested. We expended considerable assets in moving the population but only 10% of the migrant labor force was able to be saved. You can't just drop a bus load of people off in a field of wheat and expect a result."

"Combines," said Mr. Stutz. "It's the only way Robertson."

"That's where I was going with this. We need every Boeing Engineer, machinist and mechanic on a plane to Spokane in the next hour. If they can design and build a machine that flies, they can fix a harvesting machine. We need to get every piece of machinery up there working even if we have to pull them with Abrams tanks. Talk about turning swords into plowshares. The people will be dropped at every barn and processing plant up there to process and preserve the food produced. We have the smartest people in the world here in Washington and it is time to get the lead out. General, we need you to find, if you can, the nine most qualified people in the following categories: Agriculture, Petroleum Refining, Legal, Transportation, Electrical Engineering, Food Processing, Fisheries, Water, and Livestock.

No bureaucrats, we need people with dirt on their hands not lotion. We need to cut this State in half, east and west. The east will continue producing land based food while the west will look to the sea, forests and pacifying the large cities."

"Sir," said the general. "We also need to talk about command and consent. The Governor is dead and we need a new one. I have been placed under the command of the Governor. What shall we do?"

"Unanimous consent gentlemen?" I asked the other three leaders.

"So carried," said Mr. Jackson with Mr. Bujacich and Stutz nodding.

"General. These problems are too big for one man, let alone four. Consider each of us the acting Governor. I trust the gentlemen in this room with my life and Mr. Jackson through Mr. Stutz's proxy. Most times the worst decision to make is not to make one. We each have different skills to bring to the table. Mr. Bujacich will be running the fishery, has a plan and will need resources and help to pull it off. Mr. Jackson will be running the agriculture, Mr. Stutz will run the livestock while I coordinate public works. We will all need your help in communication and coordination. What I know about all these gentlemen is that none of them want the job but they are all the most capable of doing it. Each of them will need a liaison with a member of your command structure and we will have conference calls on an as needed basis to bring each other up to speed on our progress. I see our priorities as follows:

"Step 1: Get every person who has ever worked at Boeing to wherever the combines are and get them working on fixing them or devising new ones.

"Step 2: Shut down this FEMA camp. Distribute 30 days of rations to each person and load them up on anything that moves. School busses will probably all work since lord knows the State hasn't invested in education in decades. We will use the Cayuse Pass from Enumclaw to Yakima as nobody ever takes it since it is always closed. Each school bus group will be 30 people. Mayor Jackson will have to distribute the busses to each small town. I think the incentive will be a land grant program of say 20 acres per family where the existing crop is already grown. The crop but not the land will become the property of those sent to work it. The medieval English used a virgate as a land size assuming a tenant farmer needed at least 10 acres of arable land to create a livelihood and survive. Let the combines focus on the grains and the manpower focus on the produce. Washington State growers produce six out of every ten apples eaten in the United States and all those apples will rot on the trees without people to pick them. We can also barge people and goods up the Columbia River, between that and the Snake River we can get clear up to Lewiston Idaho.

"Step 3: Figure out how to transport the grain and feed to Montana in exchange for livestock moving in the other direction." Mr. Stutz asked if Interstate 90 was open through the panhandle of Idaho and the general nodded his assent. "We need a good old fashioned cattle drive. The great thing about beef is it is "on the hoof" and can walk. The Interstate is already fenced to keep deer off the roadways."

"Step 4: Mr. Bujacich needs to get the fishery open and firing on all available cylinders. We will need to set up a large processing facility in Steilacoom using any refugees from the cities or anyone who can't make the journey east.

"Step 5: For defense, we will have to figure out how to open safety corridors out of the big cities for any of the population that wants out from under the thumbs of the warlords embedded in those cities.

"Step 6: Set up main hubs at Fort Lewis, Spokane, Everett and Yakima and sub hubs in Vancouver, Bellingham, Oroville and Pullman. We will have to figure out how to perform a census and hold elections in the spring.

"Step 7: For energy we will need to figure out how to provide electricity for any food processing plants and get them fired up. We will also have to figure out how to bring the hydroelectric dams online and distributing power to the main hubs and sub hubs. We also need to get oil flowing through the Alaska pipeline and Alberta to the refining facility on Anacortes and hopefully Tacoma.

"Agreed gentlemen?" I asked. Everyone nodded in consent. "Now, who wants to address the FEMA refugee camps? General?"

"The FEMA camp is a civilian population sir so it is more appropriate for one of you gentlemen to address them," the general replied.

I looked at Bujacich, Stutz and Jackson on the screen. Each of them had their index fingers raised beside their noses and big smiles on their faces.

"Really! Are we back in college all of a sudden?" I asked incredulously. "This isn't who is buying the next round of beers."

Mr. Stutz laughed. "Whoever smelt it dealt it. This is your cockamamie plan Robertson, you go tell it from the mountain. Look on the bright side, if more than 10% of them survive you are already ahead of the former most powerful man on earth."

"Fuck you three chicken shits," I said. "You three shit birds have people to liaise with so drop your cocks and pick up your socks. General, is the head of the FEMA camp around?"

"Yes sir. He is right next door as a matter of fact."

I was ushered into the next room over where the head of FEMA was meeting with his staff. There were charts up on the wall dealing with everything from caloric intake to sewage disposal. The staff looked haggard. The general introduced me to Mr. Killmer who was a tall academic type with long grey hair tied into a ponytail and small round eyeglasses. He reminded me of the ET professor from the movie Independence Day. He shook my hand and I was pleasantly surprised to encounter a calloused hand instead of lotion.

The general made the introductions. "Mr. Killmer, this is Mr. Robertson, who is a part of the reconstituted state government. He speaks with the authority of the Governor."

"Hi Mr. Killmer, it's nice to meet you," I began. "I'll be brief. The good news is we are shutting you down, the bad news is the emergency is ongoing. Do we have any data on the 100,000 souls you are administering? Our goal over the next hour is to classify everyone in this camp into four categories. Anyone who has ever worked for Boeing as an engineer, machinist or mechanic, anyone who is an electrical engineer, oil and gas engineer, a county judge, food processing managers, logistics managers or rail line managers, anyone who can drive a bus and anyone who is ambulatory who will be further subdivided into groups of thirty keeping any family and extended family units intact. Can you process my request?"

"Sir, what is the plan?" asked Mr. Killmer.

"We are going to move Mohammed to the mountain instead of vice versa," I replied.

"You do know that has been tried don't you?"

"I do but 10% survival is better than 0% don't you think? These people are dying, they just don't know it yet. We will be better coordinated, better prepared and God willing, luckier than the Midwest and the Mississippi Delta. They tried to save everyone while we are only trying to save those that have already shown the ability to survive."

"You will have your request processed immediately. If there is one thing we are good at, it's data. Where are the refugees headed?"

"Go east young man, go east," I said with a laugh. "As soon as the data is ready we can do some algebra, I'll address the crowd and we'll get this show on the road."

I went back into the other room and saw old man Stutz and the captain still at the conference room table.

"Do you two still have your uppermost extremity inserted into your anal orifices?" I asked.

"Fuck you Robertson," said Mr. Stutz. "I have already "liaised" with the Montana boys who are driving some of their herds west. They have threatened to personally castrate me with a rusty knife if your whacky combine program doesn't work and the grain isn't delivered. The Idaho boys also want in on your rent a geek program and have offered five tons of potatoes for every potato harvester they get working. I can't help it if you are slow."

Mr. Bujacich also chimed in. "Smitty is already headed up the Columbia with a gun boat to see what we are up against and sent an insertion crew to get me the Norwegians out of Seattle. We also need to get the Westport fish processing factories back up and running since; It is more defensible from land; already has the infrastructure in place; is closer to the Columbia and a better plan than your dumb shit Steilacoom wet dream. Besides, we all want to hear your Braveheart freedom speech meets "I am Spartacus" to the masses," as he started humming *Go tell it on the mountain*...

"You two are assholes," I said. "What's next on the immediate agenda?"

"The Cities, sir," said the general. "The warlords and despots are gaining strength and the local militias will not be able to hold them back much longer."

"General Holcomb and Major Harrison, we would have to defer to your expertise in this area. What is our intel?" I asked the military men.

"From South to North, here is our intel as it stands now. There is a large gang in Olympia that came out of the Port. They are following a gentleman calling himself the Prophet. They are the group that took over the Governor's bunker and that is now their base of operations. They are a satanic cult who have brought back human sacrifices and are reported to partake in cannibalism. There are two gangs in Tacoma, one based at the Emerald Queen Casino run by drug dealers who sent the kill squad to Gig Harbor and another at the Bass Pro Shop in North Tacoma who were a biker gang and following a gentleman calling himself the Reaper. Seattle has three gangs: One in the north; the south and the east. Bellevue has one gang based out of the Bellevue Square Mall and Kirkland has another based out of Carillon Point. Everett has a group occupying the port but they are a minor gang of longshoremen and lumber mill operators. Strategically it makes most sense to pacify the Interstate 5 corridor first then work the I-405 loop to I-5 interchanges second."

"Our military doesn't have the best record in dealing with urban insurgents, General," I said.

"That is true sir. Our military is set up for old school conventional warfare force on force. We are not set up well for urban fighting or guerrilla warfare. That is why we deployed the angel teams to covertly insert themselves into the population and are taking action against small groups preying on the local populations; much like the Major's Rosedale Gardens action, knowing that a scalpel would work far better than a chainsaw. We also did not have the assets or the right enemy for full-scale engagements. These city insurgents of despots, fanatics and warlords have organized into groups of thousands holding sway over groups numbered in the tens of thousands."

"So, General, how would you deal with someone like the Prophet in Olympia?" I asked.

The Major and General exchanged glances and the General nodded.

The Major began. "The Olympia group are religious satanic zealots and are 1,000 strong under the leadership of a self-proclaimed prophet. They are terrorizing a population of around 50,000 with threats of becoming sacrifices and potentially food. Olympia is the center of a long term blue state government so there are not a lot of gun toting red necks running around town but winning hearts and minds, to quote Kennedy, shouldn't be too hard. We need a symbol and a spark to draw out the cult leadership for some assassinations and the population should take care of the rest."

"Why didn't the Governor go for this?" I asked.

"The Governor wanted a chainsaw. He wanted us to consolidate a stryker brigade out of 30 angel teams, ride into the Capitol and rid it of the cult," the general said. "We were in the process of sending out orders to do so when the bunker was breached. The Governor was the symbol of evil used by the cult to enhance membership. I counselled the Governor against this as the cult would just hide in the general population and it would be Afghanistan all over again."

"How long to plan, set up and execute your plan?" I asked.

"It should not take more than a few weeks," the Major said. "I think all we need is a man in a white smock carrying a cross; a full angel team of twenty men dressed as Templars who will burn a few cannibals at the stake while singing *"Onward Christian soldiers"*. That should bring the rats out of the nest. The good thing about prophets is that once you show them and their followers their own mortality via a few bullet holes in their heads, not a lot of others want to wear the heavy crown that leads. The 50,000 people will get a little stiffness in their spines turning lambs into lions and deal with the rest. The cultists were all branded on their foreheads in a Charles Manson looking brand after the bunker was breached so they are not exactly hard to find."

I looked at Mr. Stutz and the Captain who were both nodding. "Done!"

"And Tacoma?" I asked.

"Not quite as simple," the general said. "We were thinking of setting the two groups against each other and let them kill themselves while we wait and clean up the mess. We can quietly open some escape hatches for the population to exit to here down I-5 and Hwy 16 to Gig Harbor while their attention is focused inward instead of outward. We wait for the victory celebration of the gang champion then drop a turd in the punchbowl."

"Anything else?" I asked.

"Just your Kennedy *"Ask not what your country can do for you speech,"* Said the Major.

"Et Tu, Brute?" I said to the Major.

"Just think of the audience as being naked," he said with a grin.

I asked Mr. Killmer to come into the meeting to present the materials I had requested. He already had a power point presentation. I introduced him to the group and Mr. Jackson came back up on his monitor.

"Gentlemen. We have a current population of 97,769 in the camp. Of that number there are 1,203 Boeing representatives that fit your description, around 1,657 drivers with commercial licenses, 975 that fit your special category needs leaving us a remainder of 93,934 to be broken into 3,131 groups of 30 people. We currently have 200 FEMA busses on hand. I would suggest deploying them with your drivers to three local school bus depots we have identified where we approximate there are 100 busses in each depot. We can pre-load the busses with rations and cots and pick up passengers in an estimated time of eight minutes per bus. Based on the round trip bus time between here and Yakima we estimate it will take us 48 hours to evacuate this camp from the word go. We have already started sectioning off your special skilled groups and their families from the breakfast line as they come through."

"Well gentlemen," I said. "This is either going to end in a full-scale riot or an orderly evacuation. Do you have a plan Mr. Jackson?"

"We do. So many of the farmers are screaming for pickers since the migrant population did not arrive this year. Your people will be distributed amongst temporary worker housing, churches, granges and commercial grower complexes. The temporary worker housing is actually very nice and sanitary since after the recent immigration crackdowns, farmers had to compete for workers by offering them better and better accommodations. We will grab whatever transportation we have working and help distribute your people from Yakima. We have sent every available runner to every town and rung every church bell in eastern Washington so we can get your people where they are needed the most, putting them under expert guidance. This is a real shot in the arm for our farmers and is giving them real hope for the future."

"OK gentlemen. I hope that history is kind to us. Are we in agreement?" I asked and was answered by nods from around the room.

"OK Mr. Killmer. Let's play the national anthem, I'll give a speech and if we can find a pastor in the next five minutes, we'll close with a prayer," I said.

A microphone was set up in the conference room and we all stood for the national anthem. Mr. Killmer introduced me as the new Governor of the State of Washington and I began speaking from my heart.

"Good morning my fellow Americans and people of the State of Washington. It is with sadness that I bring you news of the death of our Governor Franks, he was killed by a cult of religious fanatics in Olympia. I am the acting Governor until such time as the immediate emergency has ended and proper elections may be held. First I will be honest with you and tell you the bad news, this camp is running out of food and only has a 30 day supply of rations. There is no resupply. I ask you not to despair as the seeds of our salvation are at hand should you have the will to rise up to the challenge and opportunity I give to you today. Each of you that embark on this journey with us will be granted the proceeds of 20 acres of harvest to feed yourselves and your families. The crops are already grown and ripe for harvest in eastern Washington. We need your help bringing in your harvest. Each of your forefathers had a dream of prosperity that brought each of you to where you are today. We need you to embrace the ideals of your forefathers to take a journey with us to create your own destiny in the world we find ourselves in. Our country is founded on the principles of freedom and manifest destiny. You have the freedom to choose your own path. I can only offer you the opportunity and tools for your own salvation. I am not going to sugar coat it, the path will be hard work but you will be working for yourselves and hopefully, God willing, you will enjoy the fruits of your own labor. The people of eastern Washington will welcome you with open arms and are prepared for your arrival. You will be supplied with 30 days rations per person and a roof over your heads at the other end of your journey. There are two options for everyone hearing this message. You may make your own way or take the opportunity we are providing to secure your own future with the assets we can make available. There is no third option. I would ask you all to stay calm and to follow the directions of the FEMA organizers. God Bless and Godspeed. I would like to turn the microphone over to Reverend John who will lead us in prayer."

"Please bow your heads. I beseech you O Lord to look out for your faithful people of Washington who embark on a journey like the Israelites before them to reap the rewards of your bountiful gifts in this your kingdom of heaven. Please give them the strength to persevere and honor their spirit in these trying times and rejoice in their dedication to your service. I ask this in the name of the Father, the Son and the Holy Spirit. Amen."

"Ok, you two asshats, Bujacich and Stutz have some Boeing engineers to talk to in the auditorium and I'll take the special projects crew after that."

"Good speech Robertson, I'm still sporting wood," said Mr. Stutz, clapping me heartily on the back.

The Captain chimed in with, "Nice touch with the preacher, I felt like Noah there for a minute and was looking for some lumber to build a boat."

The general pulled out a hip flask and offered it to me. "You know son, the first time I had to do that I tossed my cookies all over my dress uniform afterwards."

"Well," I said taking a swig of bourbon. "At least I got to do it in here and didn't need to picture them all naked. I sure as hell hope this works. Any chance you have a little coffee, some aspirin and chow, General? My arm is throbbing like a son of a bitch and I would have tossed my cookies if my stomach had anything in it."

After breakfast I was escorted over to the auditorium to watch Old Man Stutz in action. The room was packed with Boeing representatives. Stutz was behind the podium in the center of the stage.

"OK. Listen up. I want all the eggheads on the right side of the auditorium, the grease monkeys on the left and the gear grinders in the middle to stop the monkeys from giving the nerds wet willies. Figure out the most senior amongst you and send the sacrificial lambs down front." The whole auditorium started moving around and reseating. Two gentlemen and a lady came to sit in the three chairs provided. "Good. The Chinese fire drill portion of our program is now complete. Here is the mission. On the screen behind me is a picture of a modern combine. No, you don't have to make it fly. Your mission is to make it work and no, you don't have to fabricate and build it. The modern combine has two elements: The engine and the hydraulics that make the magic happen. The good news is once it is running there is only an on and off switch so all the threshing gears are either working or not working. The only adjustment is to raise and lower the front teeth depending on the height of the crop. The bad news is that all the brains of the machine and the engine ignition and electronic carburetor were wiped out by the EMP. I have loaded up the full blueprints for a typical machine you will find in these ten laptops for the eggheads. There are around 200 combines in eastern Washington and we only have a week to get them all up and running. You and your families will be flown from here to Fairchild Airforce Base, probably in a plane you built and sent to the John Deere combine manufacturing plant in Spokane. No pressure or anything but if you can't get the combines working then around a million people will die and I'll lose my nuts to a bunch of Montana cowboys. This is bush fix time boys, I don't need the air conditioning and GPS to work. I figure if you boys can make shit fly then something that mows and threshes corn and wheat should be a walk in the park. You people are the most technologically advanced and capable on the planet. Your country, State and my ball sack need you to be at your best. Questions? Yes, I see many hands in the air. Please ask these three down here because I would not understand the question or be able to provide the answer. First plane leaves in an hour so figure out who your best people are and get them on that plane."

Mr. Stutz watched the groups slowly coalesce around the team leaders each offering problems, solutions, potential issues. A few arguments were breaking out.

"Listen up fucktards," yelled Mr. Stutz. "Get your shit in one bag and get moving. You three team leaders pick five people each and get on a god damn plane. Get your hands on a combine and have a workable solution before the second plane lands. Now move!"

The auditorium emptied out quickly with a few wild-eyed glances at Mr. Stutz. Next in were the electrical engineers as I took the podium.

"Welcome gentlemen. Our asses are in a crack and you are the enema. You are going on a boat ride to the Grand Coulee dam. Your mission, should you choose to accept it, is to power up select facilities in our State if possible. If not possible then we need to know what you need to make it possible. We will stick with primary users. Is anyone in the room familiar with hydroelectric power and its distribution?"

Two gentlemen in the crowd stuck their hands up.

"OK, you sir," I said pointing to one of the gentlemen. "Quick resume please."

A short bespectacled balding gentleman stood up. "I am an electrical engineer and was the distribution manager at the switching station coming off the dam."

Another older gentleman stood up. "I worked on the turbine flow switches and step up transformers on the dam."

"Thank you gentlemen. Let's start at the beginning with you, sir," I said pointing to the second gentleman. "Please come up here and using the whiteboard give us a brief description on how the dams work."

"Well sir, the Grand Coolee is the largest hydroelectric plant in the United States. Water built up behind the dam is sent through large pipes to twelve turbines that turn and generate alternating current electricity. The electricity is created by turning magnets around a wire coil, invented by Faraday who you might have heard of, and run through what is called a step up transformer into high energy transmission lines. The alternating current and transformers were created by Tesla who you might have heard of as well. The high energy lines are used because it reduces friction as electricity passes through three hot power lines that is phased at three different frequencies. The high energy lines are run on those big steel transmission towers you see and there are four wires, three phases of electricity and one common ground wire. It is then run to distribution hubs or substations where the power is stepped down through transformers and distributed through the grid where it is dropped off at high voltage primary three phase users and further stepped down to lower voltage users like homes. Those are the cylinders you see on power poles and the green ones you see around town."

"Thank you sir," I replied. "What do you think an EMP would have done to the system?"

"Well, I'm guessing here but I believe it definitely would have fried every step down transformer in the grid depending on the frequency of the Compton effect, magnitude of the surge and the location of the EMP blast. I think the high tension lines and step up transformers would have survived because there are switches that would have tripped if any power was trying to back feed into the system. Hydroelectric power balancing is a delicate business due to fluctuations in usage on the grid. A coal or natural gas generator is either on or off. The dams were used to turn up or down the volume of energy on the grid due to their size and ability to modulate flow by turning on and off the turbines and water flow quickly. Bottom line, we can turn the juice on but the power coming out of the wires isn't usable and there is nowhere in the continental United States that manufactures transformers. I don't know if the Grand Coolee is necessarily the answer you are looking for since all roads lead to Bonneville. There are actually fourteen hydroelectric generating dams on the Columbia River but the Grand Coolee is the great regulator of the system due to its size. It can power up to five Seattle sized cities all on its own. Over 75% of the State of Washington is powered by hydroelectric power."

"Thank you sir," I said giving the man a nod. "So we can probably generate and distribute high voltage power but nobody can use it in its current form."

"Sir!" The first gentleman stood up and said, "I might be of assistance here. I ran one of the distribution hubs that tapped into the high tension system and was there when the EMP struck. The entire substation literally melted down before the shunts could stop the flow of the ultra-high tension lines' electricity. The electricity came too fast at too high a voltage, it literally melted the wires in the step down transformers; there were sparks shooting out everywhere."

"So everything downstream of the main backbone high tension system is shot?" I asked.

"Actually sir," the gentleman said. "That isn't entirely true. You see the Federal Government knew about the vulnerability of the grid and certain critical infrastructure was hardened against EMP using shielded cables and there are certain industries considered critical to national defense. The government could not replace every wire and cable in the country due to the cost but it did slowly upgrade the system over time based on the importance of the facilities. You might remember when the Alcoa aluminum plant in Bellingham had a direct feed from the Grand Coolee to produce aluminum for Boeing during the Second World War. This military base actually has its own hardened step down shielded substation as does the Tacoma refinery. Odds are that if Fairchild Air Force Base is a strategic air command or (SAC) as they are known, nuclear bomber base, then it too has a hardened substation. Boeing has one in Renton and Everett and Anacortes has one. The Army Corps of Engineers actually runs 10 of the dams on the Columbia river."

"So you are both telling me that assuming the power lines are still in the air we can turn the lights on in any EMP hardened installation in the State just by flicking a few switches?" I asked incredulously.

"Yes sir. We would have to isolate the rest of the system by turning it off so we don't start a bunch of fires but in theory it would work."

"Why hasn't it been done?" I asked.

"I have been asking the same question to everyone I can get to listen to me. I've been told that the entire Army Corps has been tasked with shutting down the nuclear plants so they don't melt down. I would imagine that Washington State, Oregon and parts of California are not high on the priority scale since all the critical hardened facilities also have generators sir. All the housing on this base was replaced in 2004 so the entire system is hardened. That's why I have been asking why I have to sleep in a tent on a cot when all they have to do is turn the power back on to the base housing."

"Thank you gentlemen," I said shaking my head. "Here is how this is going to work. You two gentlemen are now the department of energy. The rest of you now work for them. Those of you with a background in high voltage and switching, go with the dam crew while the lower voltage group go with the other gentlemen. We will get you diagrams of the grid, switching stations and substations. Your mission is to get the power up and running safely to a list of facilities we will provide you. We will work with the army corps of engineers but failing that we will get the five independently owned dams on the Columbia up and operational. Figure out a plan of attack and get after it."

Next into the room was the oil and gas group who assured us that if they could get juice, get the pipeline pumping and if the Anacortes and Tacoma facilities had not been damaged beyond repair they could fire up the plants, get cracking and start refining oil into diesel, gas and jet fuel.

Transportation and logistics were the next group. They were tasked with figuring out how to get rail lines working using steam locomotion, river barges up the Columbia River and trucking from the various hubs created. The mood of the various meetings was upbeat and optimistic that while success was not assured, they would all give it their best and were happy to be moving in any potential forward direction. My upbeat mood was soon dissipated when I saw Mr. Killmer motioning me over.

"Status report?" I asked, walking up to him.

"Sir, we are loading busses as we speak. About ten percent of the camp population chose to leave in their own direction and there is a growing group of dissidents that refuse either of the two options you have afforded them and want to speak with you directly."

"Let's grab the general and go see this crew. Do we have a judge?" I asked Mr. Killmer.

"Yes sir, the honorable Thomas Smith is waiting with the general. He is a Pierce County Superior Court Judge."

"Good, let's bring them both along."

The four of us stepped onto the marshalling yard and I was pleased to see people boarding busses and heading out behind the armored scout patrols we had already sent to secure the passageway to Cayuse Pass. There was a large group standing to the side with crossed arms and scowls pasted on their faces. I saw a large burly man who was speaking to a crowd and had the crowd nodding around him. I stepped right up to him and said, "Hi, I'm James Robertson. I understand you want to see me."

"I don't know what kind of bullshit election you held but I sure as shit have never heard of you and certainly didn't vote for you. We're not leaving. We paid for all this shit the government has here so we think it's ours."

"And you are, sir?" I asked.

"Brandon Canardo," was the reply.

"Well Mr. Canardo; that is not an option. Is there any particular reason you refuse to leave or do you just feel entitled to be taken care of by the government?"

"I have a daughter who is a diabetic and a son that is asthmatic," he said. "There is life-saving medication here for my children and I do not have the means to keep insulin refrigerated; us leaving here would be a death sentence for my children and I won't do it."

"I understand your position Mr. Canardo, I have a daughter of my own," I said. "Mr. Killmer, where were you going to send Mr. Canardo here?"

Mr. Killmer regarded his tablet. "Mr. Canardo, his daughter Cloe and son Maxwell, were being sent to the corn canning plant in Spokane. It is right next to Fairchild Air Force base where insulin and corticosteroids are available. He has been issued emergency supplies of both insulin and an inhaler for the journey and any processing time at the other end."

"Thank you Mr. Killmer," I said, turning back to Mr. Canardo who was looking at me dumbfounded. "Do we still have a problem?"

Mr. Canardo shook his head, recovering quickly. "It says in the Constitution that in times of emergency the government has to defend and take care of us. You expect me to just pick up my family and leave to parts unknown and work for the government? That is Communism and I'm not signing up for any of that bullshit."

"Well sir," I began before Mr. Smith stepped forward putting his hand on my arm.

"Mr. Canardo," Judge Smith began. "I don't know where you read that in the Constitution but you are dead wrong on all accounts. The government has a responsibility to defend our country from all enemies, foreign and domestic and defend your rights and freedoms as an individual. Nobody is forcing you to do anything except to leave this federal facility. You don't seem to have any common sense. I have heard your claim under your rights to petition the government and am now prepared to render judgement. You appear to be a danger to not only yourself but inexcusably your children as well. Your third choice is to be arrested for child endangerment, have your children removed from your custody and adopted into another family."

"Over my dead body!" he said with his chest puffed out.

"That may be the result sir. Do you have any last words before final judgement is declared?" the Judge asked ominously.

"I'll get on the damn bus but if anything happens to my children I'll personally come back here and take matters into my own hands," he said with finality.

"Sir," the Judge said. "Your recourse is at the ballot box and I encourage you to exercise that right, I'm sure Mr. Robertson doesn't want your vote. He is simply trying to keep you and your family alive and give them the best chance for survival. Now to the rest of you. You all have the right to petition your government. If any of you wish to be heard please line up in front of the large tent at the entrance to the facility over there away from the bus terminal. I will hear each of your cases but be forewarned, loser pays. If your case is adjudicated in your favor you keep your rations, if not, you lose them. If you miss your bus then another will not be provided and you will forcibly be removed from the facility or potentially shot for insurrection. Your call."

"Listen everyone," I said to the crowd. "There is no food. All the rations we have are being sent on the busses. You may go your own way and take your chances or follow our lead and take your chances. I wish you all good luck and Godspeed."

There were no takers for the Judge. He turned to me. "I sure hope you have some type of legitimate legal authority here Mr. Robertson. You seem to be getting the lead out and moving with speed and conviction so I can support that. What else do you need from me?"

"Well Mr. Smith, the President gave me and three others this shitty responsibility so welcome to the shit show. You are now the acting Supreme Court Justice for the State of Washington until you find some other judge superior to you who is willing to take the job."

"How do I get out of this chickenshit outfit, it seems you are a few loads short of a brick?" he laughed.

"Just keep us on the legal straight and narrow with the Constitution as the guiding principle and we should get through this mess, God willing. Now raise your right hand; good. Do you so solemnly swear to keep our chestnuts out of the fire, follow the Constitution and do what you are told?"

"That isn't the oath you jackass!" he stammered.

"See Tom, you're already doing your job," I said as I turned away to see the progress of the evacuation.

I put my arm around Tom's shoulders and we walked back to the command center. I introduced him to our gang of misfits while he was treated to a tirade from Mr. Stutz to Mr. Jackson.

"I did not."

"Did too."

"Did not."

"OK kids, what's the problem?" I asked looking at Mr. Jackson on the screen.

"Jackson bet me two grand your eggheads couldn't get a combine working after he's had 100 John Deere people working on it for the last two months."

"What happened?" I asked.

"The eggheads showed up with a checklist and set the mechanics to work. They torched two holes in the floor of the cab, ripped out the electronic distributer and wired up a standard V-12 distributer cap they found in an old firetruck, then they ripped out the entire ignition system and rewired the solenoid to the starter. All the hydraulic wiring and switches were yanked. It takes three of them to run it and it sounds like a dying duck but one of them starts it with a screwdriver and runs the up-down arm with the same screwdriver by manually crossing the switch points. The second one has to hold a wire in place to start the threshing gears while a third one drives it. The machinists took some measurements and are searching for some lathes and CNC machines to haul back to Fairchild to make some new switches and modify the existing carburetors. The eggheads are taking their FrankenCombine for a spin looking for some wheat to mow while the John Deere people are shaking their heads in befuddlement. Jackson here is welching on our bet."

"Does it work?" I asked with a smile.

"Don't know yet but Jackson is light years ahead of where he was. Now we are trying to figure out how to get the grain trucks working and lord only knows how we can get a grain elevator working so we can get the grain from the bins into silos but all that was moot until FrankenCombine came around. This shit might just work."

"What's next?" asked Mr. Bujacich.

"Time to go home," I said. "Mr. Jackson has the con."

"Sir," said the general in a panic. "You can't go. We are making arrangements to bring your families to the base. We need to keep the continuity of government in place now that is has been reconstituted. There are decisions to be made and progress monitored."

I laughed. "General, my wife would have you sanding a deck inside of five minutes if I let her anywhere near here. There are four of us and one will be on station at all times. We have communications available in an emergency. The one thing I know about management is put the best people you can find in place, give them clear direction and hold them accountable for the results. The best thing we can do right now is get the hell out of the way and let these people do their jobs. Manifest destiny general, it's going to work or it's not, fretting over every detail is a waste of time and energy and is often detrimental to the mission. Any of you guys want to stay other than Mr. Smith?"

"Hell no," said Mr. Stutz and the Captain in unison. "Let's get the hell out of this cluster fuck."

The dune buggies and a different patrol boat took us back to Bujacich's pier where Mr. Stutz was kind enough to drive us home. We were home in time for dinner and Mr. Stutz decided to stay. We enjoyed a meal of salmon and rice. I was only gone for a day but missed my extended family greatly. A lot of the debris from the attack was cleared and the windows were boarded up with plywood. Allison the nurse stayed over to watch over Marcus and Randy who were out cold. There were armed guards patrolling the grounds and set up in more fortified strategic positions around the house.

"What happened?" my wife asked.

"Not much," I replied. "It seems Mr. Stutz, the Captain and a gentleman over in Spokane are the new Governors of the State. We had to get the lead out of some asses and kick a few others but other than that nothing unusual."

"Well if you're the Governor then I'm the Queen of England," my wife said.

"Well your Majesty, I'm really tired and ready for bed. Want a one handed back rub?" I asked pointing at my arm in a sling.

CHAPTER 8

I woke up in the morning thinking the previous day was just a bad dream but seeing Randy grimacing at the breakfast table and plywood over my windows brought me back to reality. I grabbed a cup of coffee and sat down at the table to a hearty breakfast thinking of all the things we still had to do to prepare for winter. The Major was looking intently at a picture his daughter Ellie had drawn for him with his wife Cindy hovering at his elbow with more grits and eggs. My daughter climbed into my lap to show me her picture and was explaining the intricacies of the horse she had drawn and how she wanted a pony. My heart ached when I saw the three empty seats usually occupied by Amy and her two beautiful children. I knew that I was the intended target and they were the unfortunate victims. *It's my fault. If we had just stayed here and kept my mouth shut then none of this would have ever happened. How many people did I send to their deaths yesterday?* The dark thoughts vanished though when my daughter asked me to go play dinosaurs with her and Ellie. I was glad for the distraction, immersing myself in her innocence. *No, we are doing the right thing so my daughter can grow up in a non fucked up world.* Joy made up a plate to take to Marcus who was stuck in bed and would remain so for a few more weeks. My arm was sore but it was tempered down to a dull ache with the aspirin I took when I got up. The morning was overcast with the usual marine layer misty rain we endure through the winter season here in Washington. The Major and I took a stroll with a second cup of coffee.

"How goes it?" I asked.

"They got the Vikings out of Seattle, Stutz has the con, Mrs. Katsich has volunteered to be the interim mayor downtown. Other than that, things are moving forward. Bujacich said he defers to you and Stutz and told us he was fucking off to Alaska with the Vikings to get the fishery unfucked. His words not mine. Besides the coming of winter and some tinpot despots running around, things are OK."

"OK?" I asked.

"Look at it this way," said the Major. "What did all your prepper fiction books and estimates say about a full United States grid down scenario?"

"90% of the United States would perish," I said with a sigh.

"I'll do you one better," said the Major. "The official government estimate put together by people who actually study this shit say 92% of the population will perish in the event of a catastrophic grid down scenario. Washington has only lost 45% of its population thus far. I know winter is coming and the numbers are morbid but 92% is the measuring stick. It will come down to the will of the individual to survive. You and your team are trying to stack the deck in every conceivable way and doing incredible things the federal government didn't even think of but in the end it rests on the people, not the government."

"Thanks Major," I said. "I needed that. What do you have on tap for the day?"

"I am going hunting with my son. We haven't had a lot of time to spend together since I got back and I want to let him show me what he's learned other than how to undo a bra strap."

I laughed. "Well then, I guess I have a day of unicorns, rainbows and nail painting."

"Enjoy them while they are young, it's all downhill from here." He laughed, walking back to get geared up for a day on the trap line and hunting.

I saw Randy on the patio with Allison hovering by his side.

"Hey," I said to the two of them.

"Hey, thanks for saving me yesterday," Randy said with emotion. "Have you got a sec, I wanted your opinion on something?"

"Sure, I absolutely think you should go ahead with the sex change operation and think Shirley is a wonderful name. Have you told everyone yet?"

He laughed with a grimace. "You dick, don't make me laugh, it hurts like hell. Allison and I want to get married next week and I was wondering if you'd be my best man?"

"Congratulations you two. I am so happy for you. We would love to have Allison here with us even if she is making a bad decision."

"Well, we were thinking of moving into Amy's house if that is OK with you. It's just at the end of the driveway. I'll keep doing what I'm doing around here but we would like a little space and make a real go at building a homestead and a family. Allison does great as a nurse with Doctor Reynolds and I would like to build some more gasifiers to sell at the market. I'd have to use your tools and shop for a while until I can build my own but I'll pay you for the use of it."

"Randy," I said looking him in the eye. "You took a bullet for me and my family. You are welcome to anything at the homestead and I'll hope you would take your meals with us as Amy did. I think you will do her home proud but the neighbor is kind of an asshole and his wife is really nosy. Your dog, if you get one, better not shit on my lawn. I'd give you a hug if it didn't hurt and give Allison one if it wouldn't make you jealous."

"You're an asshole," he said, shaking his head with a smile.

"I get that a lot. How about a hug for Allison and a handshake? You'd better not tell my wife about this or it will turn into an extravaganza with the Governor there and everything. She will cost you a fortune in food, the band, the photographer, the DJ, the florist. The list never ends. Marcus had the biggest smile on his face when I married Belle since I'm sure he was happy having her off his tab and onto mine."

The Sergeant came onto the porch dressed in hunting garb.

"How they hanging Gunny?" I asked, shaking his hand.

"Still to the left sir," he said with a laugh. "I was wondering if you had a moment."

"For you Gunny, I have two."

"Well sir, we have put Bravo squad in the Black's old house and I was wondering if you have any additional greenhouse material? We would also like to put up an observation post in the tree line between the properties so we can watch both and run some communication hard lines between the Black's, here and Amy's house. The crew needs more to do and idle hands are not a good thing. Building some better defenses would keep them from painting rocks and policing the area for cigarette butts."

"Mi casa is su casa Gunny. Have at it and my thanks. Just watch out for the General, all improvements must meet her stringent guidelines for quality and aesthetics."

"Yes sir, and thank you sir."

Everything seemed shipshape at the homestead so I continued up the drive to see Ginny and the folks at the cul-de-sac. The area seemed to get better and better every day I came to see it. The laundry was all done, the seating area was scrubbed clean and the showers were now wood sided with hot water piped from a communal wood stove into the shower heads. The gardens were all cleared with chickens rooting around the area looking for morsels and any grains or seeds left in the soil. Cords of wood were neatly stacked by the fire. I saw Ginny's garage had been walled in with a double set of doors with a vestibule in between built to keep the heat from escaping. Ginny saw me through the window and gestured me to come in. The ladies were finishing cleaning up the breakfast meal and were working on preparing lunch.

"Come in out of the rain dear," she said as I entered the vestibule and entered the workshop.

"How are you my love?" I asked, giving her a warm hug.

"Wonderful dear. We're going to have a wedding next Sunday. I am so excited for Allison and Randy. He actually came to ask my permission to marry her. He is so sweet and even hooked up one of his gas machines for me. We only turn the generator on in the afternoon for our sewing and to charge all the batteries. It makes a heck of a racket so we keep it off in the morning. I heard about the attack on your house. I am so sorry. Would you like a cup of tea?"

"I would love a cup. How is your son?" I asked.

"Oh, he is very good to his family. He brings his earnings home to the family from the clinic. He is such a good provider but is very generous in what he charges, especially to those that can't pay. Alisha is still quite taken by young Jacob and they are walking out together. He is such a gentleman and will be a very good husband and provider someday. My teenage grandson is finding his way and we hope Randy will take him on as an apprentice to learn a good trade. He is not bright like his father so my hopes of medicine are probably not in the cards. It is so hard for the kids to adapt since there are not as many opportunities as there once was. I remember when I was in school you were told what you were best suited for and that was the end of it."

"What did you do Ginny?" I asked.

"I was a homemaker dear. Not one of those stay at home moms you have today, spending their days shuttling kids around and supervising the gardeners and house cleaners. We built a home for our kids to grow up in, our husbands to come home to and a community in which we wanted to live. Kids had chores and went to play with their friends until the street lights came on; everyone knew each other's names. Before the fall everyone was too busy, too plugged in and jacked up on happy pills. Truth be told, I'm glad the lights went out. It has brought our family closer together and our community closer together. We have passed each other hundreds of times over the years, exchanged a wave and hurried to the next engagement. I never knew your name. Now I know your firecracker wife, your daughter who comes to visit and even your in-laws. I think everyone has a chance to be better off in the long run, having much more appreciation for the little things and be surrounded with love. Those are the things that are important in life, not material things. I've been on this earth for 80 years and know a thing or two about love and happiness."

"I hope everyone shares your optimism and point of view Ginny," I said with a lump in my throat.

"They might not now because they are still feeling sorry for themselves but they will by the end of winter, I guarantee it. Now, be off with yourself, I have work to do and if you ever wear your boots in my kitchen again I'll give you a good hiding," she said with a smile.

"You've made my day Ginny," I said.

"Thank you for the visit, now take this tin to your wife for me. She can't have the recipe and I better get that tin back. I also expect to see you two in the near future for dinner."

"Same to you Ginny," I said giving her a kiss on her offered cheek.

I headed down to Adam's place to see how he was doing but found out from Miriam that he and his crew were out felling logs to chop up and bring to Arletta. Miriam said his crew was up to twenty cords of wood a day and looking at increasing his hauling capacity to keep up with demand. I walked back to the house and dropped off Ginny's tin with my wife who was scrubbing the kitchen clean with Joy.

"Did you get the recipe for this pound cake?" she asked me directly.

"Ginny said you weren't getting it and wants the tin back."

"Well, we'll see about that. She keeps kicking my ass at the church tea service. I think she's buying off the judges with some of her booze."

"Your grandma's tarts are pretty darn good honey but I have to say, Ginny's pound cake is a little slice of heaven."

"Don't you worry, she wants us to go up for dinner next week and I'll clean her clock at cards. She'll be in so deep she'll have to give it up."

I laughed as I started patching bullet holes and measuring windows for the scroungers to find. I have three partially constructed houses still up in Gig Harbor so I figure I can repurpose those. It almost felt like a typical Sunday afternoon if the world wasn't falling apart and all.

THE END

www.ingramcontent.com/pod-product-compliance
Lightning Source LLC
Chambersburg PA
CBHW021248170626
46808CB00011BA/2614